I0788787

CARIN HART

MY WIFE

A SLASHER DARK ROMANCE

For those who want to be the most important person in someone's life…

So important that they'll die for you.
Kill for you.

And maybe even wear a mask while they're doing it…

PLEASE NOTE

Thank you for checking out *My Wife*!

For this Halloween, I decided to write my own love letter to the slasher genre. I was inspired by one of my favorite older shows—*Harper's Island*—as well as Agatha Christie's classic whodunnit, *And Then There Were None*, and wanted to set a slasher romance on an isolated island where the 'guests' are trapped with a masked killer. Of course, there's a lot more to it than that as our heroine discovers, especially when you take in her past with Halo Island… and the husband she thought dead these last five years.

This is also a slasher *dark romance*. There are twisted romantic elements, plenty of open door sex scenes (with varying levels of consent), and a HEA that is perfect for two of the characters. Which two? Well… you're going to have to read the book to find that out. It's still pretty graphic, gory, and the masked killer pulls no punches when it comes to his kills—or Cyn's descriptions of the mess she finds as she's running for her life.

Because of that, this book includes: murder (on and off page), body horror (mutilation), prior SA (attempted forced blowjob), grief (including a funeral), death of a spouse, death of a parent, cheating, masked man/masked stalker, degradation & praise, knife play, cnc/dubcon, primal chase, PIV and anal sex, spanking, gaslighting, unreliable narrators, and a MFM threesome (including DVP).

For a full list of more detailed warnings, please visit my site. *My Wife* is a shorter novel (~60k words) that is as bloody as it is erotic, and while the hero(s) are as obsessive as any of my other MCs, this is definitely unlike anything I've ever written before.

So buckle up, and if you feel like this is something that can scratch your itch, I hope you enjoy your stay on Halo Island—because our FMC definitely will… eventually.

Happy hunting!

xoxo,
Carin

WELCOME TO
HALO ISLAND
'til death
do we part...

OCTOBER 29

THE GULLHAVEN GAZETTE

October 29   @gullhavengazette

GULLHAVEN FOOTBALL STAR GONE:
CLAYTON RIVERS, AWARD-WINNING KICKER FOR GHS, IS MISSING AND PRESUMED DEAD AFTER CAR FOUND ABANDONED.

Clayton Rivers (instagram @carinhartbooks)

Gullhaven mourns one of its own today as Clayton Rivers, 22, has been reported missing in Little Falls, New Jersey, and presumed dead based on the evidence discovered at the scene. Mr. Rivers is known to our community as the star kicker that helped lead Gullhaven High School to its first championship season five years ago. After graduating, he moved across the country...

IN THE OCTOBER 29TH EDITION OF THE GULLHAVEN GAZETTE:

GULLHAVEN FOOTBALL STAR GONE: CLAYTON RIVERS, AWARD-WINNING KICKER FOR GHS, IS MISSING AND PRESUMED DEAD AFTER CAR FOUND ABANDONED.

Gullhaven mourns one of its own today as Clayton Rivers, 22, has been reported missing in Little Falls, New Jersey, and presumed dead based on the evidence discovered at the scene.

Mr. Rivers is known to our community as the star kicker that helped lead Gullhaven High School to its first championship season five years ago. After graduating, he moved across the country because of his scholarship to Rutgers University, where he attended for four semesters before leaving to marry his high school sweetheart, Cynthia Preston. He went into securities, and used the Rivers' family wealth to create his own venture capitalism start-up, Whitewater Securities.

He was predeceased by both his father, Calvin Rivers, and his mother, Jeannie Rivers, who perished in a private plane crash in the Cascades last summer. He is survived by his wife of two years, Cynthia Preston-Rivers. At this time, the Little Falls Police Department are treating the circumstances of his disappearance as suspicious. There are also no plans for any funeral arrangements currently, though well-wishers are invited to gather at Gullhaven High School's next home game against the Avalon Lancers where the PTA will host a moment of silence for Mr. Rivers.

WELCOME TO
HALO ISLAND

'til death
do we part...

ONE
GHOSTS

ONE MONTH LATER

I'm burying an empty casket.

My therapist says this could be my way of gaining a little bit of closure. Even though my husband isn't in the mahogany box being lowered into the hole in the ground, in order to move on, I need to go through the motions of mourning Clay.

He's dead. Those two words have been repeating on an endless loop in my brain since the cops showed up at our house. At first, he was only missing and I clung to the hope that they would find him. But his car was abandoned. So were his wallet and his phone. And just to make sure that my hopes were smashed into a million pieces, I learned that there was so much blood splashed and spilled all over the driver's side of his Audi, it would have been impossible for him to survive if it was his.

I needed to believe that he did. Clay was all I had… he *needed* to be alive. But last week, the CSIs confirmed my worst suspicions: DNA results were in, and that *was* Clay's blood all over the car.

I already knew he was gone. We started dating at seventeen, and from the moment I agreed to be his girlfriend, we were never apart. We got married at twenty. If Clay was alive, even bleeding out, I absolutely believe he'd claw his way back to me.

He didn't, and now I'm a widow at fucking twenty-two.

I'm not a stranger to tragedy. This isn't the first time that I've stood at a graveside, dressed all in black, watching my whole world disappear into the ground. Five years ago, I did the same thing, burying my mother. Only she *was* in the box, and I'm not sure what's worse: not knowing what happened to Clay but 'burying' him anyway, or knowing how my mother died and not being able to change it.

At Caroline Preston's funeral, I was one among hundreds. Nearly all of Gullhaven came out to mourn her. Her fiancé, Rick. Our neighbors. Her boss at the clinic, plus her fellow nurses. Most of my high school class were there, too, but I wasn't naive enough to believe they gave a shit.

Oh, no. They came to gawk. To point. To stare. To whisper, too, and murmur to each other about what they were doing that fateful night when she died.

Everyone knew what happened on Halo Island.

Every single Gullhaven High senior was on the island, celebrating our upcoming graduation. It was a beautiful weekend in mid-May, with our teachers and a handful of parent chaperones on site to keep us from getting up to no good on the small island about fifteen miles off of the coast of California. We booked every cabin and campground the island boasted for our class of about ninety, but we all knew that the lake in the center of the island was off-limits once the sun went down.

No one was supposed to go there, but when my mom didn't return to the cabin I shared with a handful of my friends, I went searching for her. Unlike Clay, she was easy to find, bobbing face-down on the surface of Halo Lake.

They said my mother drowned herself. That she wanted to die. Why? She'd only just gotten engaged to Rick Tallows. My dad died when I was three and, until Rick came along, it was only the two of us. I was getting ready to graduate from GHS, and my mom was looking forward to spending the rest of her life with her new fiancé. She wouldn't have committed suicide, but she *did* drown.

As for Clay…

I don't know what happened to him. I don't think I ever will.

Oh, the cops say the case is open, but when I arranged for this farce of a funeral, accepting my husband was gone… I got the idea that they'd only solve the mystery of his death if the answer fell right into their laps.

My mom's funeral was crowded. Today, I'm the only mourner.

If I had Clay's body returned to me, I'd bury him in California with the rest of our families. Since I couldn't bring myself to tell anyone who knew him back home that I'd given up hoping he'd turn up alive again, I threw enough money at a funeral home to go through this so I could say it was done the next time I met with Dr. Lucas.

I'd rather tell my therapist that than discuss the unsettling feeling I've been struggling with lately. Ever since the cops showed up at my door, I just… I just can't shake the feeling I'm being watched.

It hits me now. It's November in New Jersey, and though I've lived on the East Coast for almost five years, I was a Cali girl for most of my life. I'm dressed warmly in a black sweater, black jeans, and a long black peacoat. That should be enough to chase away the chill, but as the coffin reaches the bottom of the grave, I shiver—and it's not because of the weather.

I clutch the single red rose I'm holding tightly, grateful that the funeral director sheared off the thorns. He's a stern man in his early forties who met me at the grave before disappearing to give me privacy once the cemetery staff member started to lower the empty casket. I'm supposed to toss the rose on top of it once he's done, a symbol of saying goodbye to my husband.

I'll never say goodbye to Clay. If that means I'll take

this rose home and press it between two pages of a book, I will—but, first, I turn to see if someone really is watching me.

There never is. Whether it's the alley between my neighbor's lot and mine, or the shadows of our backyard, I never actually see someone there when my senses are tripped… but now?

I *do*.

My heart skips a beat when I spy a very familiar man waving at me once I notice he's there. He has on a sleek black leather jacket—probably the only piece of black clothing he owns—and a pair of dark denim jeans. Aviator sunglasses hide his deep blue eyes, and he steps lightly in his heavy boots, purposely moving around the recently covered grave plots as though he can't bring himself to disrespect the dead.

Thomas Gillis.

What is he doing here?

His tousled black curls waft in the November breeze. He shoves his hands in the pockets of his jacket, his expression turning from friendly to sympathetic as he moves to join me by the graveside.

He gives me that old, familiar, crooked smile. "We've got to stop meeting at funerals."

That's right. The last time I saw him, it was during another tragedy. Another funeral. Clay's parents both perished when their private plane went down over the Cascade Mountains in California. Their bodies *were* recovered, though they were in no state to have an open-casket funeral, and me and Clay flew out West for the first time in years to make all of the arrangements for the Riverses.

Tommy was there. It was awkward for all of us, especially when he noticed the ring on my left hand and casually asked if his wedding invite got lost in the mail. The truth was that Clay and I eloped without telling any of his family—since I had none—or any of our friends. But Tommy showed up at the funeral to support Clay, and I know I shouldn't be *that* surprised he's here now.

But I am. I can hardly believe he's here, and for a simple reason, too: I didn't tell anyone except Dr. Lucas, Detective O'Halloran, and the funeral home I hired that I was 'burying' Clay.

I drift closer to him, forcefully swallowing the lump that lodged in my throat when I initially recognized him. "Tommy. You came."

Tommy removes his right hand from his jacket, flicking his sunglasses up so that they're nestled in his mess of curls. His gaze sweeps over my face, taking in the deep purple bags under my eyes, plus the tight smile I can barely offer him.

His hand lands on the shoulder of my coat. "Clay was my best friend. I had to."

Even after everything that happened, Tommy still thinks of Clay as his best friend. I haven't shed a single tear since I arrived at the cemetery earlier, but that realization has my eyes stinging.

It's true. Clay and Tommy were incredibly tight when

we were kids. Even in high school, they were loyal friends who did everything together… and that included eventually falling for the same girl.

Me.

I still have my regrets about how that all went down. When my mother died, I was only six months away from turning eighteen. I could've returned to my childhood home, but the idea of living in it alone gutted me. Especially with graduation only a couple of weeks away, I had to stay in Gullhaven. I just didn't know where.

Tommy wanted me to come stay with him. It made sense. We'd been in a committed relationship since freshman year when boys started looking less like friends and more like boyfriends. He was mine, and we were so serious that, by the time we were on the cusp of graduating, the town gossips were making bets on how long before he popped the question.

Then my mother drowned on Halo Island, and everything changed…

I couldn't stay with Tommy. Besides his mother being a bit of a prude—no mixed-sex sleepovers at the Gillis house, which just meant Tommy and me snuck over to mine to fuck—there was also the fact that he had one younger brother and two younger sisters. It was too full of a house for me; I was used to being an only child with a single parent. But Clay…

Clay had both of his parents at home, but that only meant the big Rivers mansion was their address. So busy with work and building their wealth and reputation, they were rarely there. Clay convinced them that he didn't need a live-in nanny by the time he was thirteen. At seventeen, he ruled the entire place on his own.

He didn't have to ask his parents if I could stay. The three months I lived with Clay in his family home, I think I saw them twice. They smiled, thinking I was Clay's new girlfriend and, well, by the time summer ended, I *was*. We were foolishly, desperately in love, and I had to make a choice.

I had to break Tommy's heart and admit that, while his best friend was doing his girlfriend a favor, they fell for each other. When Clay left for New Jersey at the end of August, there was nothing keeping me in Gullhaven. I followed him there, and we'd lived together ever since.

But that big house in Gullhaven… it's one of the reasons that, when we moved to Little Falls, we bought a decent-sized two-floor house instead of a McMansion. With Clay's money, we could've afforded something much larger, but that's not what he had in mind. When he wanted to be with me every moment he could, there was no reason for us to have more than a handful of rooms.

Now they're all empty. He's gone, and like how I put my mom's house up for sale without ever spending another night inside of it, once this burial is over, one of the first things I'll be doing is looking for a good real estate agent.

At least, that was the plan. Now that Tommy's here…

"How did you know?" I ask him. For him to fly out

just in time… "About the burial today. I didn't tell anyone."

A flash of guilt dances across his face. It might've been five years since I was his girlfriend, but I've always been able to read Tommy. "You sure you want to know?"

I squeeze the rose's stem so tightly, it nearly snaps. "Yes."

He holds up his hand. "Okay. I don't want you to think I'm stalking you or anything, Cyn, but when news got back to us at home that something happened to Clay… how you sounded when you called… I didn't want to bother you for updates. The cops wouldn't talk to me because, shit, why would they? So I set up an online alert. Any news that might've popped on Clay's case, I'd get a message sent to me."

That's pretty smart, actually. Considering I feel like the LFPD has been giving me the runaround, I should do the same thing.

"Anyway," he continues, "I got a notification three days ago. Clay's name was on this funeral home website, saying there would be a private burial for Clayton Rivers today. I figured, even if you didn't want to invite any of us, I could still come, hide out in the crowd." His gaze darts around the empty graveside. "That obviously didn't work, but I'm even more glad I came. No one should have to mourn by themselves."

Fuck. *Fuck.* Those tears stinging my eyes from before? They begin to spill over.

Tommy Gillis, man.

I blink them back. After how much I hurt him when we were kids, I don't deserve his sympathy. I sure as hell won't stand here and cry, grieving over the man I cheated on him with, all while Tommy joins me as the only other mourner.

And then he smiles again. There's pain in that smile. Heartache. Matching grief.

Two warring thoughts dash through my mind: *I'm so fucking sorry*, and one of the things my devoted husband said to me time and time again over the last couple of years…

Clay loved me. I don't doubt that one bit. When we got together, we both lost Tommy, and despite my three-year relationship with him, Clay gave up his lifelong best friend when he chose a happy-ever-after with me.

I feel so fucking cheated. He promised me forever, and all we got were five short years.

He wouldn't have left me. Someone took him from me, and if I ever find out who, I'd kill them myself. I really would. He was my life, and now that he's gone, I don't know what the hell I'm supposed to do.

Tommy knows. Murmuring words of sympathy, saying all the right things that people who go to the funeral say even when those truly shattered by the death don't want to hear it, he lets me surreptitiously wipe away my tears as I realize that this is it. This *is* goodbye.

My husband is gone, and I'm little more than a ghost.

The wind cuts through me. My long blonde hair blows all around, and I wish I would've pinned my hair up. I didn't because Clay liked it down. He liked it long. It was something small I could do, and as I shove my hair out of my face, I don't even think about taking a hair tie out to pull it back in a ponytail.

When I don't respond to Tommy, he falls silent. I crave the quiet. His presence at my side does help, and I'm not sure if it's because I'm not alone—or because it's Tommy fucking Gillis who is standing mere inches away.

Our hands brush. An electric charge rushes through me, and I take a hurried step away from him.

Tommy clears his throat. "What's your plan now, Cyn?"

I blink at him, not comprehending what he's asking me.

"You know. Clay… he's not here anymore. There's nothing keeping you in New Jersey." He hesitates for a moment. "Is there?"

Only the fact that Clay died here and I don't think I could ever truly move on with my life if I never find out what happened to him. Is that enough of a reason to stay? I'm going to sell our house; that's non-negotiable since I can't stay there any longer without seeing my husband *everywhere*. But I don't have a job here. I didn't want one, and Clay was more than happy to have a stay-at-home wife. Because I rarely left the house, I didn't make new friends. I don't even have a pet. I could pick up and leave as soon as I decided to… but where would I go?

I shake my head, and Tommy answers my unsaid question.

"What about home?"

"Gullhaven?" Is he serious? "You think I should move back to California?"

"I mean… yeah. Cyn, I know you left because of what happened to your mom—"

I turn my head away from Tommy. "I don't like to talk about that."

"I get it. I *do*. But Gullhaven is home. I'm sure you have good memories there, too."

I fell in love with Clay in Gullhaven.

I fell out of love with Tommy in Gullhaven.

He moves closer. Through the late autumn temperature, I can sense his body heat reaching out for me. "You have friends there, Cyn. Not for nothing… you have me."

Damn it.

I shift on my heel, tilting my head back so that I can meet Tommy's gaze. It's guarded, and I know how much it costs him to admit that—in his way—he still cares enough about me to make that offer.

Just like Clay thought he might.

"Clay always said…" Another lump lodges in my throat. It's so hard to get the words out. "He said…" I shudder a breath out through my nose, struggling to hold onto the last shred of composure I have. Every time I think I'm all cried out, the tears sting my eyes once more and I'm proven wrong again and a-fucking-gain.

Tommy takes my hand, squeezing it. "I know, Cyn."

I told him that night I called Tommy and told him Clay was missing. When the panic gave way to icy numbness if only for a few moments, I managed to utter the words in a flat voice. *If anything ever happened to him, get Tommy. Call Tommy. Go to Tommy. He'll be there for you.* Clay told me that, and I told Tommy, and when he swore he'd be on the next flight out to Newark, I hung up the phone after I refused his offer.

But he didn't listen, did he? Oh, he gave me my space this last month, but now he's here… and Clay told me to turn to Tommy if I needed help.

He's *not* here, but if there's one thing I've always done, it's listen to what Clay told me to do—for the most part.

Gullhaven.

Can I really return to Gullhaven?

And, if I do, will the rumors that chased me out of the small coastal town all those years ago be there to welcome me home?

There's only one way to find out—and I don't think I can do it… until Tommy moves to stand next to me, our shoulders touching, and I experience the first sense of peace since the cops knocked on my door.

For the first time since Clay left me, I'm not alone.

WELCOME TO
HALO ISLAND
'til death
do we part...

TWO
GOOD NEWS

FIVE YEARS LATER

"Cyn? You home?"

Home. It's so hard to believe it, even after more than a year of us living together, that this is my home—and I share it with a man who looks for me every time he walks through our front door.

"I'm in the kitchen," I call out.

Seconds later, there he is. His curls as wild and attractive to me now as they were more than a decade ago, his handsome face thinned out a little from his boyish looks, and his toned body undeniably belonging to a man. His sculpted arms play peekaboo with me beneath the uniform polo shirt he wears down to the office every day. It's good publicity for him, too. When you go to your physical therapist, you want him to look like he takes care of himself.

And, at twenty-eight, Tommy Gillis still takes excellent care of his body. Trust me. As his partner for the last two years, I know every inch of him intimately.

I turn the knob on the old gas range down so that the pasta doesn't boil over, then turn to meet him in the middle of the kitchen.

Tommy palms my ass as I go up on my tiptoes to kiss him in greeting.

"Have a good day?" I ask, bracing his chest with my hand.

"Always do when I know I'm coming back to you," he says, deep blue eyes twinkling as he runs his hand down the curve of my ass cheek. "Something smells delicious."

"Garlic bread," I tell him. "It's in the oven. Once the spaghetti is done, I'm going to toss it in sauce and melt some mozzarella over it." A comfort dish from my childhood and, considering the date creeping closer and closer, I needed some comfort tonight. "It's almost done, but you're early. I wasn't expecting you for another half an hour."

"Got some good news and wanted to come right home to tell you."

Oh? My stomach twists a little even as I pull a smile on my face. "This wouldn't have anything to do with how secretive you've been lately?"

Tommy waggles his eyebrows. "Maybe." He laughs a little. "Damn. I thought I was being sneaky. You noticed that?"

I shrug. "You've been on the phone a lot. Coming

home later than your usual time instead of earlier. If I didn't know better, I'd wonder if you were cheating on me."

You'd think I'd tiptoe around the topic. If I had to spend the rest of my life *not* addressing the elephant in the room, I never would've started over with Tommy. Between the both of us, we decided to keep the past where it belongs: behind us. We were only seventeen, after all. Tommy wouldn't hold my getting with Clay before I actually ended things with him against me as long as adult Cyn gave her word it wouldn't happen again.

He has nothing to worry about on that front. Just like I know that Tommy will never, ever fumble his second chance with me.

And in case I needed reassurance?

His easy-going expression takes on a hard edge. "Never." His voice drops an octave lower than its usual tone. "You know I would never do that."

I do. "So what's the good news?"

That settled, Tommy's impish smile returns. "You know how I was talking about maybe doing something for Halloween?"

I nod. It's another thing he and Clay had in common, their love for the holiday. Over the years, Tommy's younger siblings—in their late teens and early twenties now—all grew out of it, but there was something about the magic of monsters and horror films and candy that

Clay enjoyed until his death, and that Tommy gets excited over every year.

I wish I could match his enthusiasm. But considering what happened a couple of days before…

I try. It's tough, but I try, and I keep an open mind as Tommy tells me what he's been planning for ages now.

"Okay. So I had this great idea, right? It was hard, getting the week-long slot I wanted for us all, but I got a call from the new owners right before I came home. Halo Island is open to rent from next Friday all the way through Halloween."

Halo Island. That name is a punch to my gut. No, no, no. He's not suggesting what I *think* he's suggesting… is he?

Oblivious to the way my heart just about stopped beating, Tommy continues. "From the 25th until November 1st, we get to be one of the first ones to see the new and improved camping set-up on the island." He's almost bursting with excitement now. "It's glamping or some shit, but it still sounds like it'll be fun. A secluded wooded island on Halloween where we're alone? Awesome, yeah? What do you think?"

What do I think?

I think I'm going to puke.

Do I go pale? I'm pretty sure I just went pale because, suddenly, Tommy's hands land on my shoulders.

"Hey. Cyn. You okay?"

I don't know. A nervous tic of mine, I duck out from under his hold and immediately start twisting the narrow gold band on my left hand as I ask myself the same question. *Halo Island*… am I okay?

Tommy sees me fiddle with it, but he doesn't say a word about that.

We both know why I still wear Clay's ring. I give Tommy everything I can, but that was the line in the sand I had to draw when we got back together. I couldn't bring myself to take it off, and if that was a dealbreaker for Tommy, it was better that we got that out in the open before we both ended up heartbroken this time around.

He said he could deal. So far, he's held true to his word. But when I'm twisting my ring, it's a dead giveaway that I'm not in a good space mentally—and he knows it.

I've been so good lately. I actually did what Dr. Lucas suggested before I left New Jersey: I moved on. I never meant to, didn't really plan on it, but after five years glued to Clayton Rivers' hip, I knew I needed to figure out who Cynthia Preston was without him. I dropped my married name because it was too painful to be Clay's when he was *gone*. The house sold within a few months of me putting it on the market, and since Tommy was in constant contact with me, putting the bug in my ear about moving back to Gullhaven, I finally did.

Of course, he needed to help me settle back in. He helped me find an apartment of my own when I point-blank refused to move into his 1950s-style ranch house with him. He reintroduced me to the friend group I had years ago, and before long, it was like I never left.

And after three years of Tommy being my bonafide emotional support human, allowing me to lean on him while I navigated a life without Clay, he finally suggested we give *us* a second try.

I say three years. Tommy tossed the idea at me the first time about a year after I relocated to the West Coast, and I did everything to ignore him. For fuck's sake, part of me kept thinking that Clay's death was just a sick joke. That he'd pop up one day, trying to figure out why I wasn't waiting for him in Little Falls.

But years passed, and though that strange, unsettling feeling that someone was always watching me never went away, my desperation to be reunited with my dead husband ebbed enough that I could look at Tommy and think… maybe.

Maybe I deserve to be happy. Maybe I deserve to be loved. Clay said that, if anything ever happened to him, I should rely on Tommy. Though I really doubt that Clay had any idea that something *would* happen to him, I took his words to heart. I let Tommy back in.

And now, look at us. Last year I *did* move into his house. Now we're like an old married couple, exchanging a kiss in the kitchen while I prep dinner for when he gets off of work.

The only difference is that, while I have a wedding band on the fourth finger of my left hand, it's not Tommy's. We're not married, though that's not for lack of trying on his part, and when I struggle, it's Clay's ring I cling to.

Boy, am I struggling at the moment.

Halo Island.

Why would he bring me back to Halo Island?

I swore I'd never go back. After they sent a Coast Guard boat out to ferry my mother home in a body bag, I promised myself I'd never return to Halo Island. It would've been easy to keep that promise, too. Besides the fact that I ended up in New Jersey, Halo Island itself was shut down after my mom drowned.

Halo Island has always been privately owned. So much smaller than any of the other islands off the coast of California, the guy who rented out the cabins and campgrounds decided it wasn't worth the risk after my mom died during a high school trip she was chaperoning. Last I heard, he was tearing down the old structures to dissuade locals from visiting, and the ferry from Cottonwood Harbor stopped heading there.

But that was years ago. After that, I stopped paying attention. On the rare occasion anyone mentioned the island around me, Tommy usually ended the conversation before it inevitably touched on my mom's suicide. Because, in Gullhaven, something exciting so rarely happens around here that the locals need to gossip about awful fucking things that took place a damn decade before.

I didn't know it was reopened. I had no idea that it was a glamping getaway for people who could afford to buy peace and solitude, a week at a time.

Until now.

Tommy explains it to me, eager to get me to agree. It's a group excursion, but we'd have our own cabin, complete with electricity, a fridge, and running water; the 'glamping' part, I guess. Only those in the group get to be on the island, though, and we'd have to bring everything we need for the week we're there. The ferry drops us off on an assigned date, picks us up on an assigned date, and since the whole idea behind this getaway is to unplug, unwind, and get back to nature, there's no cell service on the island. No internet. No cable television or streaming, though there might be an old-fashioned DVD player in our cabin. No stores, either, just the bonfire pit, the renovated cabins, and the lake to entertain us.

More importantly, it'll just be us, and I'd have to be a heartless bitch to refuse when Tommy obviously put so much time, effort, and money into planning this for me as a surprise.

Only… he couldn't have picked a worse week for this trip.

I'm still quiet, and his mood shifts.

"We don't have to go, Cyn," he says softly, his enthusiasm suddenly waning. "If you don't want to… if you *can't*… I'll call the whole thing off. Yeah, I'll lose the deposit, but I don't give a fuck. I still have the week off of work. We can spend it here together, just you and me."

And then I'll feel guilty *and* sad the entire time.

No.

No.

I swallow roughly. "Do we need to stay the whole week? Or is the weekend good enough?"

No matter what, I can't be away from home on the 28th. That's the day my world split in two: Clay and No Clay. The cops showed up at my door on October 28th, and whatever happened to my husband, that's the day I mourn him the most.

Halloween is on a Thursday this year. The 28th is Monday. I can give Tommy Friday through Sunday. Monday morning at the latest if I have to.

Relationships are about compromise, right? I'll go. I can't promise I won't have a fucking meltdown, returning to Halo Island for the first time since my mother died, but I'll go… so long as I don't have to turn my grief into a performance for Tommy and his friends on the 28th.

I know that's not what he intended. Tommy would never do that to me, and I think he realizes that his attempt to distract me might've been done in good faith, but I'm not ready to pretend October 28th doesn't have meaning to me.

"We got a deal for the whole week, but if you want to leave Monday morning, I can arrange for the ferry to take us back as soon as the sun's up. Everyone else can stay without us. What do you think?"

When I nod, Tommy visibly relaxes. I don't think I realized how sure he was that I would react poorly to his 'good news' until I agreed to at least return to Halo Island for a couple of days.

In as pleasant a mood as he was when he first walked

into the kitchen, he sidesteps around me, moving toward the counter where I was prepping the rest of dinner.

It hits me a second later what he said: *everyone else.* Right. He mentioned it's a group getaway.

"So, who else is coming? Who did you invite?"

He pops a piece of the mozzarella I chopped into his mouth. "Everyone."

Everyone, huh?

Yeah. I need a little more information than that.

WELCOME TO
HALO ISLAND
'til death
do we part...

THREE
DISTRACTION

Gullhaven is such a small town, we know everyone—and everyone's business, too. Our graduating class had less than ninety students; one reason why we were able to have our seniors' weekend on the island. Since I moved back, I've noticed that Tommy's friend group isn't that much different than the one we all had as kids. The stereotypical 'popular' clique made up of three football players, the high school newspaper editor, a pair of cheerleaders, the class clown, and, well, Chase.

I start ticking off names. "You. Me. Summer and Tyler." When he nods, I immediately say, "Madison," because Summer doesn't go anywhere without *her* emotional support human. "Vee." I raise my eyebrows. "Aaron?"

Tommy nods. "They're both stubbornly determined

not to let their recent break-up mess with the group's dynamic."

I get that. That's the thing about growing up in a small town. We partner swap. *A lot.* Me dating Tommy for nearly all of high school only to start dating Clay right as we were getting ready to graduate was almost expected, and it wouldn't have been a big deal if I'd broken up with Tommy first. Just like how Summer had a few months' fling with Tommy before getting back with her on-and-off-again boyfriend, Tyler. With the exception of Tommy and Clay, I'm pretty sure Madison fucked anyone who ever wore a GHS varsity jacket—both while we were in school and after, and considering the whispers around town, she's still doing it so long as the guy says he's on the right side of eighteen.

Vee was with Aaron in middle school. Ignored the flirtatious troublemaker all through high school, then gave him a second chance once he seemed to calm down a little in his mid-twenties. They got back together about two years ago, right before I gave Tommy a second chance. I figured they would be the next to get married after Summer and Tyler, but Vee ended things over the summer.

Since then, she's been cozying up to Chase Whitmore. Nothing serious, just a couple of nights out together that they both claim aren't dates, but I can't help but not believe a word out of *his* mouth, at least. After all, I know how good of a liar Chase is.

No one believed me at all when I told the group that

he shoved my head in his lap and wouldn't let me up again unless I blew him.

Well, no. That's not true. Tommy believed me. So did Clay. I was still dating Tommy when Chase tried to force me to suck his dick after he—drunk and stupid and super horny—yanked down his pants and, with his hand on the back of my head, forced my face into his lap. Though Tommy and Clay were outside, playing beer pong, when I got trapped by Chase on the couch, I went right to my boyfriend after I bit Chase on his exposed thigh and escaped him. I had to beg Tommy not to beat the shit out of Chase then and there, and that was only because I didn't want him getting into trouble at the height of base-ball season.

Even before Clay was into me as Cyn and not just Tommy's girl, he offered to slug Chase for me. Our star kicker, I refused to be the reason he lost his scholarship to Rutgers. Besides, when Chase came strolling out onto the back patio with his pants back on and my bite mark hidden, he laughed it off, pretending like I got it all wrong. That he'd never make a move on his buddy's girlfriend.

I was too sensitive. I couldn't take a joke. I thought he was serious? Nah… he'd never do that.

And, except for my boys, everyone believed him. By the time we were back in school, rumors ran that *I* tried to make a move on Chase, that I was the town slut who would suck any dick that got shoved into my face. When

Chase turned down my offer, I made up a lie so that Tommy didn't dump me on the spot.

That was ten years ago and I still don't know who started the rumor—though I can guess, and if Tommy has his way, I'll be spending a whole weekend with her on Halo Island. As for Chase…

I hated him for what he did to me *and* my reputation. For the next couple of weeks, I refused to go anywhere unless Tommy was glued to my side, and if Chase was going to be there, I'd rather stay home. School was the only exception, of course, but other than that? I would've done anything for the rumors to die down.

Then, about a month after that party, Chase got jumped on his way home by who he claimed were a couple of kids he pissed off from the town next door. He was beaten so badly, he spent the rest of senior year both in the hospital, then a rehab center in Southern California where he had to regain the use of his legs after they were both broken. Supposedly, he found God after that, even thinking about going to seminary school, though he ended up following in his father's footsteps by becoming a lawyer.

Shocker, right?

Finding out that Tommy and Chase are still good friends all these years later was almost a dealbreaker for me. Only knowing that Tommy never once downplayed what Chase did got me past it. None of that 'he was just a kid' bullshit, or 'he changed'. Tommy fully admits that

Chase was a predatory asshole then, and a power-tripping dickhead now.

Why are they friends? For the same reason that I smile and pretend like Summer is one of mine: because we grew up together, and even if we're all in our late twenties now, none of us have really shaken that high school mentality.

Since me and Tommy got back together, I've actually spent more time around Chase than I ever did back in high school. We have this unspoken agreement not to bring up the past—one I wish I had with Summer—but that doesn't mean I like the idea of spending a couple of days so far off the mainland with him.

So I hold my breath and ask, "Chase?"

Tommy moves until he's next to me, then gooses my side. *Yes.* Damn it.

Then he says, "I'll make it worth it, love. I promise," and I forget all about Chase as I instantly tighten up.

Tommy pats my hip, a silent apology, then lets go of me as he heads toward the stove.

It wasn't the possessive grab that triggered me, though. Once our relationship turned intimate again, I expected Tommy to be handsy with me. He always was, and in so many ways, he hasn't changed one bit from the fifteen-year-old who nearly creamed his pants the first time I let him put his hands under my shirt. Tommy touches me as often as he can, almost as though checking to make sure that this is real, that we are together again, and I don't mind that.

But *love?* Tommy's not big on pet names. He prefers to use a nickname, if anything. In fact, he's the one who started calling me Cyn in high school instead of Cyndi—my name all the way through middle school—or my full name, Cynthia. Clayton became Clay. Our friend Violet is Vee. The only one who ever calls Tommy Thomas is his mother, even though he turned twenty-eight last month. It's just how he is.

And then, a couple of weeks ago, he called me 'babe'. It just slipped out. We were sitting on the couch, watching TV together, when I got up to get some water. I asked if he wanted any, and he nodded and said, "Thanks, babe."

That was what Clay used to call me. I was his 'babe' or 'baby', and the second Tommy used that name for me, grief washed over me. I stumbled, head whipping around as though I'd find Clay leaning back on the couch instead.

My face gave me away. I never had to tell him why it fucked me up to have him call me that. He knew, and that was the last time he said it. He's started referring to me as 'love' instead, and because I'm trying so hard to keep my head above the grief I've spent the last five years treading water in, I let him have it.

Tommy loves me. No denying that. There are moments when I catch him looking at me out of the corner of my eye and wonder if he ever stopped. Obviously, our relationship is completely different than it was a decade ago. We're both adults now. I'm a widow, and while Tommy glosses over his dating history, he's too handsome, too kind, too charming not to have plenty of girlfriends after I left him the first time. He loves me now in a more mature way than he ever did, and as much as I can with part of my heart still belonging to Clay, I love him.

Does that mean I can handle how easy it is for Tommy to tell me so? He was the first to actually say the words—*I love you*—and when I couldn't right away, he promised me he would wait as long as it took for me to reciprocate his feelings.

I finally did. On the one-year anniversary of our second first date, I told Tommy I loved him. The words stuck in my throat, but they've come easier and easier since.

Now two years have passed since we've been together again. I can't tell if he's planned this getaway only to help distract me with Clay's death anniversary coming up so soon, or if he has ulterior motives...

A weekend on Halo Island with our old friend group —including a couple of my high school tormentors. It's Tommy's found family, and a chance to build new memories… *better* memories on the island.

I grew up. I moved on, remember? Chase is going to be there? Summer? I can handle that, especially if Tommy wants them to join us for some reason.

And if I'm pretty sure I know what that reason is…

As Tommy stands in front of the stove, giving the spaghetti a quick stir before removing one of the long strands, testing it to see if it's done, I lean against the counter and thumb the metal of my wedding band.

Shit.

I knew this might be coming. Tommy's so honest, so *genuine*, that it was also inevitable. He's been dropping hints, too. Talking about how it was a shame that Clay and I eloped, that I deserved a real wedding. He asked me about my favorite flowers—lilies—and mentioned that, while moving in with each other was a start, he was ready to take our relationship to another level.

Like, oh, marriage maybe?

The anniversary of Clay's death is like a dagger in my chest. It is every October, and I've grown to dread Halloween since it's only a couple of days after I first learned that Clay was gone.

Is that Tommy's plan? Get me to Halo Island at the end of October with all of our friends and ask me to marry him?

What would I say?

Part of me still thinks of myself as Clay's wife. I'm Tommy's live-in partner, too, but there's a reason I've never been able to take my wedding band off. So what if Clay's death means that the 'til death' part of our vows had been met? He's still my husband, and I'm not sure I'm ready to have another one.

I'm not sure I'll *ever* be ready to.

Tommy knows that. I made it clear when we first got together after he let me cry on his shoulders for three years that, if he wanted to be more than friends, he had to accept that there were limits to what I could give him. He promised he did.

Did he change his mind? Or does he mean it? That this is our way to reclaim Halo Island?

I promised myself I would never go back.

But I love Tommy Gillis, and if he really wants me to join him for the weekend on a secluded island with people I can't stand most of the time, I'll do it.

For him.

After everything he's done for me, he deserves me putting in a little effort.

WELCOME TO
HALO ISLAND
'til death
do we part...

FOUR

COTTONWOOD HARBOR

Halo Island might have gotten a glow-up since the last time I was there, but Cottonwood Harbor is just as rickety as I remember.

My hand tightens on the handle of my rolling suitcase. I have a backpack on, too, because I couldn't fit all of my toiletries into my luggage. Tommy has his own duffel bag, smaller than my backpack, that he assures me has enough clothes to last him from today until Monday. It's slung over his dark blue hoodie, secured while he pulls the oversized cooler behind him.

It's stuffed full of food. Without anywhere to grab a bite on the island, or even a small shop to pick up groceries, each of us going on the trip decided we'd bring as much as we thought we'd need, and then we'd share. Tommy might not have packed more than three pairs of underwear—unlike my seven because, well, you never know—but he's made sure we won't starve during our getaway.

I eye the narrow platform that's built about ten feet past the ocean's shoreline. It's been standing for as long as Gullhaven's been a town. I know it's carried thousands of people to and from the boats and ferries parked along the edge, but something about the way it's *creaking* in the late October breeze coming off the Pacific has me hoping the cooler isn't *too* heavy.

The saltwater-crusted harbor isn't the only thing that looks like it's seen better days. The ferry that's waiting for us along the front of the harbor is the same exact one that brought half the senior class of GHS to the island, including me and my mom. The paint along the side—claiming the small ferry as *Mulligans' Mariner*—is faded and peeled. I see visible dents toward the front of the boat. The bow? Stern? I don't fucking know, and I really don't trust that dinghy to take us the fifteen miles out to the island.

But I have no choice. I agreed to this, and there's only one way to get there: that boat.

Tommy told me that the new owners of Halo Island made an agreement with old man Mulligan, one of the OG ferry operators who work out of Cottonwood Harbor. No other boats are allowed to dock on Halo Island due to the exclusivity nature of the agreement, and Mr. Mulligan will take as many trips out to the island and back as necessary during our booked week.

That doesn't mean we can head to the mainland

whenever we want. The trips must be scheduled with the ferryman ahead of time. That's how I know that Violet and Chase chose to take a later ride after they were done with work while the rest of us chose the afternoon slot.

It's quarter to two now. I see a heavily highlighted head of dark hair already stalking around the edge of the ferry like she owns the fucking thing. Behind her, a tall, willowy woman with wavy, sandy-colored hair hovers right there.

Looks like Summer and Madison already beat us to the harbor. I don't see anyone else, though. Where's Tyler? Or Aaron? Aaron's usually late, and we're a little early for our two o'clock departure. But what about Summer's husband? Unless he's on the other side of the ferry or something with Aaron—

"Shit."

I glance over at Tommy. While I'd been staring at the boat, he pulled out his phone. "Something wrong?"

He frowns down at the screen. "Aaron just ditched us."

"What? You mean he's not coming?" I didn't get a buzz on my phone. Even though I know there's no service on the island, I brought it with me because, well, it's habit. "He cancel through the group chat?"

Once I agreed to this when he sprang it on me two weeks ago, Tommy set up a group chat specifically for those of us who were taking the trip. It made it easy to discuss who was paying for what, what time we should meet at the harbor, if anyone else needed to leave early like Tommy and I did, and what we were bringing for food. As of this morning, everything seemed good to go, and the last messages I received were from Summer and Madison, showing off the matching set of nails they got for our trip.

Summer got blood-red on her inch-long nails. Madison went for adorable little pumpkins drawn on her much shorter ones. Violet apologized for not being able to make the appointment the night before.

I painted my own nails black because, well, I wasn't invited, was I?

Tommy shakes his head, curls rustling gently in the breeze. "Nah. I guess, since I'm the one who set up the weekend, he sent the message straight to me. Here. Look."

AARON M

Hate to drop this last minute on you, bro, but I'm not gonna make the ferry at all today. I picked up a chick at the bar last night and she's still with me. Gonna spend the weekend with her. Maybe the week, too, if I get super lucky.

Tell everyone not to have too much fun without me.

I snort as Tommy slips his phone into his back pocket. Same old Aaron. "I'm surprised he didn't try to get her an invite so he could shove her in Vee's face."

"Maybe it's for the best that he's a no-show. Don't forget. Vee and Chase both used the work excuse for why they'd take the ferry over later. If they wanted to be alone before we even got there, I'd hate to shove *that* in Aaron's face. Watching your friend get with the girl you loved… it fucking sucks, especially when you know she was better off without you."

Oof. Looks like Halo Island might be stirring up some bad memories for both of us. For me, it marked the night my entire life changed when my mom died. For Tommy, it was the beginning of the end of our high school relationship.

I'm clutching my suitcase with my left hand. With my right, I find Tommy's. "I'm here now."

And if we both know that I wouldn't be if Clay hadn't died, Tommy is so horrified at what he just said, he doesn't mention it.

Instead, he squeezes my fingers. "Cyn, I'm so sorry. I didn't mean it."

Yes. He did. But he didn't mean to make me feel guilty for things that happened in the past that I can't change. Since I've reconnected with him, he's never brought up our past in such a way, and as his eyes dart over my face, checking for my reaction, I know he'd take back his words if he could.

Letting go of my suitcase, I cradle his jaw, rubbing my thumb over his scruff. The simple kiss on his lips is my way of accepting his apology. He sighs against mine, murmuring my name.

I draw away. "Come on. We don't want to miss our ride."

His next exhale is one of relief. "Right. Let's go."

MULLIGAN—ALWAYS JUST 'MULLIGAN'—HAS BEEN running this ferry my whole life. When I was a kid, taking random weekend trips to the island with my mom before its lake stole her from me, he seemed ancient. That's nothing compared to now.

His hair is white. His face is made up of wrinkles so deep, his watery brown eyes are easily hidden among them. The faded blue cap with the embroidered *captain* on the front is frayed along the brim. He walks with a slight stoop, but as Tommy and me board the ferry, he takes my luggage from me without any trouble at all.

"That makes four of you'se," he says, his voice cracking as he adds my case to the much larger stash that has to belong to Summer and Madison. "Find a seat if ya like. We'll be getting underway in a minute or two. Then I'll make sure to finish your party with the last three."

Four of us. Tommy. Me. Summer. Madison. Chase and Vee are coming later tonight, and considering even someone like Mulligan could see that Tyler and Summer have been having marriage trouble lately, I guess he decided to take the evening trip apart from her. Did Aaron actually show a hint of maturity by calling down to the harbor and canceling his ride in favor of his booty call? I guess so, unless he got in touch with one of the others to do it for him.

It's possible. I've always been on the outskirts of this friend group. If it hadn't been for Tommy asking me out freshman year, I wouldn't have been part of it at all. Summer and Madison have always been besties, and Vee lived on the same street as Tommy growing up. Tyler and Clay were on the football team with him—running back and kicker to Tommy's quarterback—and Aaron came with Vee, just like I was a package deal with Tommy. And Chase…

When you're rich, good-looking, and arrogant, you just weasel your way into any group you want, I guess.

Five years away from them didn't make it any easier for me to rejoin the group. Summer takes every chance she gets to remind me that I left Gullhaven, and as her echo, Madison says the same shit. Of all of Tommy's other guests, these are the last two I'd have picked to take the ferry ride out to Halo Island with, including Chase— and isn't that saying something?

But I'm here for Tommy. He wants to give me new memories, *better* memories of the island. It's only three days. I can do this.

I *can*—

"Tommy!"

Summer finally notices that we're on the ferry. Madison nudged her, Summer looked over her shoulder, and with a squeal, she beckons him over.

Not me. Just Tommy.

He waits for me anyway. I wave him off, taking my time removing my backpack to add it to the pile of luggage. He gives me an apologetic grimace—because as much as I try to hide how much Summer annoys me, I'm no saint—before joining Summer and Madison at the railing.

I watch as Summer squeezes my boyfriend to her, kissing him on the cheek. "I'm so glad you invited us. It'll be like old times' sake again. All of us together, hanging out on Halo Island like we did when we were kids."

Tommy lifts his hand, ruffling his hair. "That's the plan. It's been so long since it closed down. I never thought we'd ever go back."

Still holding onto Tommy's arm, she glances down the ferry, making sure everyone knows she's looking at me. "I wonder why that was."

Bitch.

Ten years later and she still wants to blame me for the Gullhaven teens losing their favorite hang-out because my mom died there.

Tommy frowns, turning to search for me. Whether he did it on purpose or not, the way he shifted his upper body broke the connection between him and Summer. Taking advantage of that, he steps a few feet back my way. "Come over here, Cyn. We'll sit up front so we can see the island approaching."

From behind him, Summer scowls at me. She only does it because Tommy can't see her, something I know all too well since her pretty face snaps into a simpering smile once I tell him I'll be right there and he turns again.

The two women each grab one of his arms, dragging Tommy to the front row of bench seats near the front of the ferry. They maneuver him so that he's sitting between them, leaving no room for me on the bench.

I let my backpack drop on top of Tommy's cooler. Mulligan's disappeared, probably getting the ferry ready to go, and I think about taking a seat inside. It's already chillier out on the water than I thought it would be, but instead of grabbing a sweater from my suitcase, I hug myself and take the end spot on the second bench seat.

Almost immediately, Tommy stands up, climbing over his bench so that he can take the seat next to me.

The stink face that Summer makes when Tommy rejects her and Madison brings out my mischievous side.

"Where's Tyler?" I ask as sweetly as I can. "I know Aaron had to cancel, but where's your husband, Summer?"

"He's busy with work," Summer answers, sharing a quick look with Madison. "He's coming later with Vee and Chase."

And that makes seven.

"Great," cuts in Tommy. "I was thinking we could have a bonfire tonight, celebrating our return to Halo Island. I brought stuff for s'mores in my cooler."

Summer gives a half-hearted nod and another pointed glance toward Madison.

Summer's guard dog sets her sights on me.

"It's so nice of you to worry about Ty, Cyn, but you don't have to. Summer knows where her husband is."

Madison tosses her hair over her shoulder. "Can you say the same?"

I recoil as if slapped, slamming into Tommy's chest. Wow.

Wow.

This wasn't the first time Summer's sicced Madison on me when she was too high and mighty to land the blow herself. But, *fuck*. That was a direct hit, and we all know it.

Tommy's hold on me tightens, sudden fury in the way his muscles tense and coil. "Madison. What the fuck?"

She bats her eyes innocently at him. "What?"

"You know what."

"It was a simple question," Summer says, jumping to Madison's defense as if she hadn't given her attack dog a silent command to go after me.

Tommy's not buying it. "Please. You both know that was uncalled for. Shit. We haven't even left the harbor yet. If that's what Cyn has to look forward to from you two, maybe I made a mistake. Maybe this should've been a couple's vacation instead of one for the group."

He explained to me why it isn't. With Clay's anniversary this week, he thought it would be a much better distraction if I was surrounded by so many of our friends. If it was just him, would I be able to forget what I lost enough to enjoy myself and make those new memories he wanted me to have so badly?

Is he regretting that now? Oh, yeah.

And that makes me feel even worse.

I can handle Madison Powell. Summer Kaye, too. Their catty comments and mean girl attitudes just cover up how jealous they are that, if only for a little while, I got out of Gullhaven. They never did. Summer settled for a man she tolerates, Madison is the town tramp with a taste for barely legal boys, and I didn't just find love with Clay. I found it with Tommy, too, and they can't stand that he forgave me and took me back.

I guess, if they're miserable, they want me to be miserable, too.

For that reason alone, I lay my hand possessively on Tommy's chest. "It's fine."

His jaw goes tight. Tommy's always been my protector. He nearly broke his throwing hand, punching the brick siding of his house, back when I wouldn't let him confront Chase on my behalf; if I hadn't been with him when Chase got his ass kicked, I would've thought he was the one who did it, he was that pissed at him at the time. He only resumed their friendship after Chase recovered, as though deciding he'd paid the price for trying to sexually assault me. I haven't had any problems with the lawyer since, and anytime Summer and her underling started shit with me, Tommy was there to slap them down.

Just like he did now.

I know he thinks it's not fine. That he's debating if he should kick them off the ferry now and cover their part of the cost. Considering we have Aaron's cut to worry about already—and while Tommy does well as a PT, he doesn't have Clay's kind of money, and I can't access any of his assets until he's been declared legally dead in two years—I'd rather not do that. Plus, Summer and Madison already hate me. Why add more fuel to the fire?

I rub his chest. "Seriously," I say, lowering my voice. "I mean it. You got me on this ferry, Tommy. Let's enjoy ourselves."

Purposely ignoring the other two women, he drops a kiss to the top of my head. "I already told the guys we get the farthest cabin since I got us the slot. We'll have all the privacy we want, but if you want a middle one so everyone can hear it when I make you scream tonight, just say the word."

I duck my head against him, trying to hide my sudden smile. I don't doubt him one bit. It's one thing to know that Tommy and I live in the same house. We haven't gone away with the others since we got back together. Maybe these two need a reminder that Tommy Gillis is mine.

Then again, I'm not the type of woman to share.

"I want privacy," I murmur into his shirt.

He runs his fingers through my loose hair. "Anything you want, love. I'll give you everything you want."

I kiss his chest, then straighten up just in time to see Summer leaning into Madison. She whispers something to her, but I couldn't care less what it is.

Let them talk shit about me. I'm used to it.

Snuggling against Tommy, I do my best to ignore them as the ferry begins to cut its way through the water.

Looks like there's no getting off for any of us. For better or worse, we're all going to Halo Island together.

After a few moments of heavy silence, Summer shifts in her seat so that she's partway facing us. "Sorry, Tommy." Tommy again, I notice. Not *me*. "Madison was just teasing. Right, Madi?"

"What? Oh. Yeah. Sorry, Cyn." Oh, look at that. I *do* get an apology. "I was only pointing out that we miss Clay, too. Gullhaven's not the same without him. He should be coming on this trip."

But he can't. Because he's dead, and after the way these two spread rumors that I was the reason my mother drowned herself all those years ago, I'm not particularly surprised that they also want to blame me for Clay's disappearance.

True, they've never come outright and *said* it. If they did, I could justify cutting myself off from the rest of Tommy's friend group. He wants to believe they're my friends, too, and I've done everything I can to let him, but when they pull shit like that...

They've never accused me of killing Clay, but they don't have to. In Gullhaven, when tragedy follows you around like a dark shadow, so do the rumors.

And I'm sick and tired of trying to outrun them.

That's why, as I cozy up to Tommy again, enjoying the spray of the ocean on my heated skin, I decide that this weekend?

It's time to finally stop running.

WELCOME TO
HALO ISLAND
'til death
do we part...

FIVE
HALO ISLAND

Halo Island is fifteen miles out from Gullhaven. I don't know how fast this clunker of a ferry is traveling, but we're docking on the island about forty minutes after we left the mainland.

Cottonwood Harbor is at least a century old. The dock that Mulligan idles his boat in front of is brand spanking new. It looks a lot sturdier, too, wide and welcoming.

Just beyond it, I see a wooden sign with gleaming white block letters painted in the center:

WELCOME TO
HALO ISLAND

My heart jolts as I read it. Halo Island. I swore I'd never go back—and here I am.

It's not a very large island. About twenty-five square miles total, what makes the island so unique is its shape. Almost a perfect circle when seen from above, there's another circle of water about two and a half, three miles inland. Technically, it's fed from the Pacific Ocean surrounding the island, but the mainland locals all call it a lake since that's what it looks like from the edge of the circle. It makes the whole island itself seem like the shape of a narrow donut—or a halo.

You'd think that its holy name would mean it was a good omen. For most of my life, it was. I came to summer camp on this island. We threw a couple of ragers whenever Clay's parents wouldn't notice the obscene rental charge on one of their cards. And, of course, Gullhaven High hosted its annual senior celebration here.

Now, as I face the haunting beauty of the dark sand, the angry autumn waves, and the looming leaves on the evergreen trees that cover nearly every inch of the island, all I feel is a sense of dread.

Tommy could tell. Instead of trying to psych me up, telling me how much fun this weekend is going to be, he just kissed my neck, squeezed my fingers, and told me he'd start unloading our luggage onto the end of the dock.

He knew I needed a few minutes alone to prepare myself to face the ghosts of my past.

One ghost in particular.

Caroline Preston.

Except for Tommy, my mom was my best friend. She was only twenty-three when she had me, and barely forty when she drowned. Grief is strange. It's a terrible thing because, just when you think you can live without the person you lost, something tiny will remind you that you no longer have them. A song. A scent.

An island.

Moving away from California helped me deal with my mom being gone. After Clay disappeared, it was leaving New Jersey and the memories we made there behind that allowed me to bury some of that overwhelming pain. I thought it would get easier with time, and it has. I won't say that it hasn't. I can go days without thinking about my mom now, and though Clay is still constantly on my mind—especially in October—I do my best to think of the good times we had.

If I didn't, I think I'd go insane.

Sometimes, when I swear I catch a glimpse of someone watching me out of the corner of my eye, I'm pretty sure I already have.

You know what's an excellent motivator? *Spite.* When the last thing I want to do is give Summer fucking Kaye more ammunition to lob against me, I'll hold my head up high and walk down the dock as if it isn't costing me something with every step I take.

For Tommy, I tell myself, pushing away from the railing. I'm doing this for Tommy.

All of our luggage is gone. Summer and Madison's,

too. They must've unloaded the whole pile while I was staring at the island because all that's left is Mulligan standing by the gangplank, worrying his frayed hat in his hands, waiting for me to disembark the ferry.

"Oh. Sorry. I'm coming."

"No need to be, lass. It's good for an old man to wait sometimes."

Not when that old man looks like he's about to keel over any second now. "Thanks for the ride over." Shit. Am I supposed to tip him? Considering my wallet is in my backpack—same as my phone, just in case—I don't have any money to give the old ferryman. I only hope Tommy already thought of that. "I'll see you bright and early Monday."

"Monday?" he echoes. "Beg your pardon, miss, but I'm not scheduled to ride back until next Friday. November 1st, that's what it says on my calendar. Eight for Halloween. One Friday until the next."

Right. That's what Tommy initially scheduled. Then Aaron backed out, so we're seven, and I only agreed to come at all if we left no later than the morning of the 28th.

"That's true for most of the group," I tell him. "But there are two of us who need to cut our trip a little short. I was told it would be okay if we got a ferry ride out on Monday instead."

"Sure, sure. That's fine with me. I'll make a note of it before I start heading on back."

"Thank you."

As I start to descend onto the gangplank, Mulligan whistles. "Good thing you told me. I'm the only way on and off the island. You'd have been stuck until next Friday otherwise."

Right. Because there's no way to contact the mainland from Halo Island once the ferry's gone.

Only one problem: *I* told him.

Why didn't Tommy?

BY THE TIME I EXIT THE GANGPLANK AND TAKE MY FIRST steps on the island in more than a decade, I'm not even thinking about that. Maybe it slipped his mind. Maybe he forgot to tell Mulligan. It doesn't matter. Mulligan promised he'd pick the two of us up at the island's small dock first thing Monday morning.

Besides, as I look around for Tommy, I see his head bowed toward Summer, listening to something she's saying to him. Her hand is resting on his bicep, tugging him closer so he can hear her.

Over the waves lapping at the shore, I can't.

Damn it. I know how handsy Tommy is. He's just a friendly guy, and he thinks all of his friends are the same. Summer and Madison touching him, grabbing him, pulling him along… that's just how they are.

I know better.

I like to think I'm not the jealous type. Tommy gives me a lot of grace about our history, and I try to do the same for him. The biggest difference is that Tommy and Summer didn't have their fling until after I had broken up with him. I can't say the same for how my relationship with Clay began.

It was only a couple of months when they were both seventeen. Tyler was a year ahead of us in school. He'd already graduated, so had Vee, and the only reason they were on Halo Island for the seniors' trip was because we were all still close and they found their own ferry ride over so they didn't miss out. We had chaperones, but not as many as we should've, and a couple of locals joined us that weekend.

My relationship with Tommy wasn't the only casualty of my mother's death. By the time I ended things with him, admitting I was with Clay, Summer and Tyler broke up for the countless time. Only instead of them getting right back together, Summer and Tommy started going out.

It didn't last. By the time Christmas rolled around, Summer was back with Tyler, and I refused Tommy's offer to spend the holidays with his family. Me and Clay had our own mini celebration in his dorm room that year, and until his parents' funeral, we never went back to California.

I shouldn't be jealous. Summer married Tyler when she was twenty-three—they just celebrated their fourth wedding anniversary last May—and, for the most part, they seem happy enough.

So why can't I shake the feeling that she's trying to steal Tommy from me?

Even worse, that old haunting sensation that someone's eyes are on me has the tiny hairs on the back of my neck standing on end as my sneakers sink into the damp sand. I slap my hand there, trying to quiet the unsettling nerves as they take root in my belly. Glancing around, all I see are the trees rising up from where the sand turns to dirt and grass.

To my right, a path is cut through them, leading to the area where the campgrounds and narrow cabins used to be. According to Tommy, they're more like mini apartments instead of wooden shacks with bunk beds like they used to be, but I won't know until I follow that dirt strait to where they are.

To my left, an area is cleared for the bonfire pit that Tommy mentioned. It's made up of burnt logs and ashes from the last visitors to the island, plus a fresh stack that I saw Mulligan unload himself before setting back off for Cottonwood Harbor to wait for the rest of our group.

And in front of me, Summer is still murmuring to Tommy. His duffel bag is strapped to the front of his chest, my flowery pink and peach-colored backpack slung over his arm, while my rolling suitcase and the cooler are by his boot. Summer's mound of luggage is gone. Knowing her, she probably sent Madison on ahead with it so she could have a few stolen moments alone with my boyfriend before her husband arrives.

I trudge my way toward them, kicking up the compact sand in a tiny hint of rebellion as I go.

Whether it's the plopping of the sand falling or my shadow stretching out to them that catches her attention, I'm not sure, but Summer's head pops up. Her lips thin when she sees me. She pats Tommy's arm before stepping away and turning her back on me. By the time I'm within reach of him, she's halfway into the woods.

I jerk my thumb in her direction. "What was that about?"

"Just Summer trying to smooth things over. She's so used to you being the bigger person and not rising to her bait, I think it freaked her out when I lost my temper on the ferry."

I love how Tommy calls that losing his temper. He's usually so laid back and chill that, for him, that *was* losing his temper.

"It's Summer," I tell him, like that explains everything. And, well, it *does*. "Once Tyler gets here, she'll be too busy trying to show us all how happy they are together that she won't have time to needle me."

Tommy gives me his crooked grin. "Do we need to put on an act so everyone knows that I'm head over heels for you?"

My heart melts whenever he shoots that smile my way. Though I rarely have anything to smile about when the cloud of grief hanging over my head becomes so thick, I'm nearly choking on it, somehow Tommy manages to eke a tiny returning one from me.

I squeeze his bicep, erasing Summer's touch from the fabric of his hoodie. "If they didn't know how crazy I am about you before this trip, they sure will by the end of it."

Something flashes across his face, darkening his deep blue eyes. His smile doesn't waver, but I know what I saw. I just… I can't read it, and that's not like Tommy at all. I almost get a hint of anticipation. Like he's looking forward to this weekend in ways I can't understand just yet, and as his eyelids droop, his gaze going heavy, I remember my suspicion from a couple of weeks ago…

"Ah, Cyn. You have no idea how fucking happy it makes me to hear you say that."

Well. If he has an engagement ring tucked in his duffel bag, I think I have a pretty good idea, after all.

Letting go of Tommy's arm, I reach for the handle of my luggage. He makes a noise in the back of his throat, but while he is as gallant as he is kind, and he likes to pamper me like a princess whenever he can, I do have some limits. I'm not about to walk up to our cabin empty-handed while Tommy lugs the cooler, my suitcase, my backpack, and his duffel bag.

Jesus Christ, can you imagine the kind of snotty comment Summer and Madison would have for me then?

"The cabins are that way, right? I can't wait to see where we'll be staying for the weekend."

"I saw pictures. The owners told me they don't do the modern cabins justice, but I thought it looked great already. I'm sure you're going to love it, too." I'm glad one of us is. "Trust me, love. You're going to have the best weekend of your life. I promise."

On Halo Island? I doubt it.

Three days, I tell myself as I fall into step alongside Tommy. Friday night, all of Saturday, all of Sunday, and a ferry ride out at sun-up on Monday.

How bad can it possibly be?

WELCOME TO
HALO ISLAND

'til death
do we part...

SIX

THE LAKE

The answer: not bad at all… so far.

I don't normally like being wrong. In this case? I'll make an exception since, hours after I stepped onto the island while battling feelings of dread and trepidation, I'm actually kind of enjoying myself.

Summer hasn't made another snide comment since the ferry ride. Like I thought, having Tyler on the island has done wonders to put her in a better mood, and with her husband to distract her, I haven't seen her sidle over to Tommy once. Even now, she's sitting on the log opposite mine and Tommy's, sprawled out on Tyler's lap, her hands buried in his dark blond hair as they catch up on their day apart. They look so cozy together, I almost wonder if I'd imagined all of the nasty looks she gave me earlier today.

It wouldn't be the first time I saw things that weren't there.

Without her best friend commanding her attention, Madison was left on her own. She won't usually start shit unless Summer tells her to. On her own, her default mode is one step past flirtatious. Simply put, Madison will want to find someone to fuck, and with both Tommy and Tyler taken, she's set her eyes on Chase.

Chase Whitmore is too handsome for his own good. Clay will always be boyishly good-looking to me; immortalized at twenty-two when he disappeared, his All-American boy next door looks are how I remember him. Tommy is effortlessly attractive, with his five o'clock shadow, messy dark curls, and crooked smile. Chase's appearance screams moneyed lawyer. Everything, from the tailored shirt and khaki pants he has on—his idea of casual vacation wear—to his three-hundred dollar haircut is expensive, but beneath the veneer, he has model-handsome features. Chiseled jaw, a slight divot in his chin, high cheekbones, and 'fuck me' hazel eyes.

Pity that, when I look at *him*, all I see are the red-rimmed eyes of a drunken teenage boy who was stronger than I thought as he held my head down…

I have to say, I did expect him to sit with Vee instead of Madison. There's no denying that Vee's been spending more and more time with the lawyer lately, and while she claimed she needed his professional services, something seemed off about the untouchable businesswoman.

Violet Lee is just as gorgeous as Chase, only everything about her is natural. She wears her straight black hair short, hitting chin-length, showing off the striking cut of her jaw. Her eyes are dark, her skin flawlessly golden, and as a hobby marathon runner, her body is enviable.

She's currently stretched out on her own log, nursing the margarita she made in her solo cabin before joining us outside.

Tommy is sipping on his beer, the neck of the bottle nestled between two fingers on his left hand. His right arm is slung over my shoulder, tucking me against his side as the crackle of the bonfire flames echo all around us.

The three guys set it up after we all unpacked and got settled in. I put all of our supplies in the provided fridge, grabbing a can of soda for myself. Everyone else is enjoying themselves with a drink, but while I'll have some wine every now and then, I feel like one of us needs to stay sober, especially with the large fire burning in the pit.

The sun's gone down. This far out from the mainland, stars sparkle above our heads in the night sky. The fire drowns out the soft murmurs of conversation, while most of us are just enjoying our peaceful first night on the island.

I'm content. The first hour on the island, I was on edge. Seeing our pristine cabin with its three rooms—front room/kitchen, bedroom, and bathroom—that was actually bigger than the apartment I rented when I first moved to Gullhaven made me feel a little better about being here. It has a front door and a back one, both that lock with the key Tommy has in his pocket.

For privacy, I guess, since one of the main selling points of booking a week on Halo Island is that we have the whole damn place to ourselves. We don't have to worry about other guests or locals sneaking into our cabins because there aren't any. But with Chase claiming the cabin nearest to the one Tommy picked for us, part of me is secretly grateful for the ability to lock up when we go to bed tonight.

That won't be for a while. Each of us grabbed food for dinner in our own cabins earlier, with Tommy carrying out the supplies he brought with him to make s'mores if we get hungry again. He forgot to bring something to skewer the marshmallows on, but Madison grabbed Chase by the hand, tugging him into the woods to find some sticks.

They came back ten minutes later, Madison wiping her smug lips, and Chase's shirt just a little more wrinkled than it was before. Both empty-handed, they claimed they couldn't find any sticks in the fucking forest. Vee had rolled her eyes, walked off to her own cabin, and returned with two long fondue forks she found in her kitchen.

As she speared a marshmallow with more force than was necessary before jabbing it into the fire, I can't help but think that the sharp prongs would make an amazing weapon.

Once Vee licked the last of the white, stringy, melted

goo from her lips, she relaxed back onto her log, sipping the last of her margarita.

Madison brushed something off of Chase's folded collar, giggling under her breath.

Tommy turns his head, kissing my cheek. I can smell the beer on him as he does, but he's nursing the first bottle, simply enjoying having me right next to him.

It's cozy. The fire is a blast of heat, knocking aside the chill from the ocean behind us. It's actually a little *too* warm, if I'm being honest, and I nestle the bottom of my ginger ale can in the sand so that I can push back the sleeves of the sweater I tugged on before I came out here.

The motion catches Vee's attention. Sitting up, she announces, "It's hot as fuck out here."

I gesture at the flames.

"Yeah, but you know what I was thinking? We should go for a swim. Cool off in the water."

Tommy chuckles. "Ocean's right behind you, Vee. Knock yourself out."

"Swim at high tide in the Pacific, Tommy? With sharks out there? You must be joking. No," Vee says, waving her hand toward the woods flippantly. "Let's go to the lake."

My stomach twists.

Tommy goes still.

Summer shifts on Tyler's lap, sitting on him with her back to her husband, facing the rest of us on the other side of the bonfire. "Did someone say we should go to Halo Lake?"

The lake.

It wasn't really the island itself that I didn't want to see again. I have wonderful memories of my time here… but Halo Lake?

It's what's called an incursive lake. A body of water that's nestled in the center of the island, its circular shape makes up part of the design that gave Halo Island its name. The lake is about twelve feet deep in its center, and unlike the shore, there are no tides. No waves. It's peaceful and serene and, tucked away in the middle of the island, it's incredibly private.

It's also where my mother died.

Ten years later, I can still see the scene vividly. It was mid-May. The weather had been gorgeous all afternoon. Our gym teacher brought a pair of volleyball nets and set them up on the sand. We held an impromptu volleyball tournament—Tommy and Clay's team winning, of course—and built a bonfire to roast hot dogs for dinner, marshmallows for dessert.

The temperature dipped as the sun set. Too chilly to take a swim even if the lake wasn't off-limits after curfew. Everyone knew that you were risking the chance to walk at graduation if you broke any of the three rules: no swimming after dark, no starting a fire without adult supervision, and no swapping bunks once yours was assigned. That last one was to keep guys and girls from intermingling, and considering that just meant a handful of students snuck out to fuck where they couldn't be caught, it didn't really work.

The lake was different. Us seniors knew better than to go into the ocean at night, and even if we tried, two of our teachers set up tents on the sand to keep an eye on the shore. Because the lake was a hike to get to, none of the chaperones set up near it. The threat of possible expulsion was supposed to be enough to keep us away.

I would've. I didn't have any intention of sneaking out and walking all the way over to the lake that fateful night. By mom…

When I saw her floating on the lake, I didn't want to believe it was her. I recognized the purple blouse she was wearing, clinging to her soaked skin. Her hair—a paler shade of blonde than mine, turned dark from the water—was loose, wafting like a cloud in front of her. The tendrils barely moved since the lake itself was so still.

She had her shoes on. I remember that detail so vividly. The expensive heels Rick gave her, that she told me she'd wear when they got married at the courthouse later that summer… she was still wearing them when the Coast Guard came and dragged her body out.

I was the one who found her. I didn't know what I was supposed to do, and for longer than I want to admit, I stared in horror as she bobbed on the surface of the lake, just out of my reach. It was only when Clayton Rivers—Tommy's best friend… he was just Tommy's best friend then—stepped out of the woods, saw my mom drowned and me in shock, that I knew it was real.

It happened.

My mom *died*.

Later, Clay would admit he was sitting on the back porch of the cabin he shared with Tommy and a couple of the other guys on the football team when he saw me sneaking away from mine. I'd been worried that my mom hadn't come back at curfew, so I went searching for her. Clay didn't stop to grab Tommy. He simply followed to make sure *I* was okay.

And I wasn't. It took a long, long time until I was again, and Clay had a lot to do with that. He was the one who held me that night as the shock wore off, denial settling in just as quickly. He was the one who walked back to get help when I couldn't leave her, even though we both knew my mom was too far gone to be saved, and who retrieved Tommy for me after news broke and everyone came rushing toward the lake to see what happened.

Then, when I needed a place to stay, I moved in with Clay. And whether it was trauma-bonding or what, I started to see him as more than just Tommy's best friend.

He became *mine*.

Now he's gone, too, and just the thought of going anywhere near the lake where my mom died without the man who saved me back then…

I should've known better than to agree to this. Of course someone would suggest we visit the lake some. time during our stay. I'd have put money down on that person being Summer, not Vee, but Madison and Chase have already nodded their agreement, while Tommy rubs my upper arm.

I look at him.

His eyes are bright. Not from the alcohol, either, but the excitement of continuing the night near Halo Lake. "What do you think, love?" he asks me. "How about a swim?"

Fuck. Tommy wants to go.

If I refuse, he won't argue. He'll simply knock back the rest of his beer, tell everyone good night, and come with me to our cabin. They'll all know I'm the reason he cut the night short, and whether I have valid reasons or not, they won't care.

So I go with a flimsier one.

"I don't know. I didn't bring a bathing suit."

"So what?" asks Vee.

"None of us look like we did when we were seventeen, Cyn. It's fine. Don't be a prude. Let's skinny-dip." Summer's gaze finds Tommy. The bonfire's flames flicker in the dark depths of her irises as she smirks at him. "Unless Tommy's afraid you might trade him in a second time." Her smirk turns cruel as she looks at me again. "Got a taste for lawyer?"

Madison narrows her gaze at me, scooting closer to Chase while he just chuckles and shakes his head.

I imagine grabbing Summer by her long hair and shoving her face into the fire the same way Chase yanked me against his erection that night.

"Funny, Summer," I say, my tone making it clear that it isn't funny at all. "But I've never been interested in

Chase. Sorry." I lean against Tommy's side, stroking his chest possessively. "It's this guy for me."

"Yeah, but that's only because——"

I can only guess what kind of bitchy response Summer had in mind for me that's only cut off when Vee claps her hands, rising up from her log.

"I want to swim. Come on. Last one to the lake has to cover the bill for that deadbeat ex of mine."

WELCOME TO
HALO ISLAND
'til death
do we part...

SEVEN

SPLASH

Walking into the lake is easier than I thought it would be.

I almost chickened out. When everyone else agreed to grab towels, plus our useless phones for flashlights, before taking the thirty-minute walk toward the lake, I hesitated on the log as Tommy and Tyler started to extinguish the bonfire. By the time we were ready to go, I'd gotten so sick of Summer's sly taunting expression, daring me not to join them, that I said 'fuck it' and went.

I drew the line at skinny-dipping. I stripped down to my panties and bra, a facsimile of a swimsuit, and waded into the chilly water before I lost the nerve. Standing on the edge, staring at the surface… that would've been a lot harder than dunking under and swimming out past the point where I found my mom.

Tommy's right there with me. Like me, he kept his

boxers on. So did Chase. Surprisingly, Madison went into the water fully dressed. She must've had a tank top on under her hoodie, plus the pair of tiny shorts she was wearing while we were sitting around the bonfire. After tossing the hoodie to the shore once we arrived at the lake—Chase pulling up the rear as he ogled Madison's—she's playfully splashing him in his bare chest as the lake water molds her thin tank perfectly around her tits.

No bra, I notice, not even a little surprised by that.

Thankfully, my underwear is black. Black bra. Black panties. It looks as scandalous as you can imagine beneath the moonlight, but at least it's not see-through. I'm the kind of girl who will show off for her man. *Only* her man. With the others nearby, I didn't feel comfortable stripping down.

Vee, on the other hand…

I nudge Tommy as she floats on her back a few feet away from us. Her eyes are closed, black hair fanning out along the serene water of the lake, nipples hard as they point toward the sky. Like Summer, she stripped completely out of her clothes before diving in, her naked body on complete display beneath the moonlight.

To his credit, my boyfriend glances at her, then looks down at me as though he barely noticed she was completely undressed.

"Think she's still pissed at Aaron?" I murmur. "Or is this show for Chase?"

If it is, it's not working. With Madison giving him all

of her attention, Chase hasn't said a word to Vee since they stepped off the dock with Tyler.

"Little of column A, little of column B. Or there's a third option."

The most likely one. "Vee just doesn't give a shit what anyone thinks."

"Bingo."

I like that about her. She's never cared, and I envy her ability to just not give a fuck. If none of us had agreed to join her at the lake, I have no doubt we would've found her here like this anyway.

Of the group, Vee's the only one I really consider a friend. Sure, she was Tommy's first, but over the years, we were close. It used to be me and Vee against Summer and Madison, and though she's too busy running her online jewelry empire these days—turning her small business into one that grossed more than six figures last year —I'm glad she's here. At least, between Vee and Tommy, I don't feel as outnumbered.

We're standing in a shallower section of the lake. It covers my tits, reaching just under Tommy's pecs. I'm glad Vee's on her back. Seeing her face turned up toward the sky makes it easier to remember that she's floating, not bobbing, and that her eyes are closed because she's relaxing and not dead.

Dead.

Dead—

Splash.

I glance over my shoulder, rolling my eyes when I

notice what made that splash. While Chase and Madison are flirting openly on the other side of the lake, Tyler and Summer have drifted out a little further in the opposite direction. All the earlier splashes came from the first two. Now?

Summer has her arms over Tyler's broad shoulders. The former running back is even bigger at twenty-nine than he was at nineteen, and strong enough to clutch his slender wife to him, making her ride him while holding her up and partway out of the lake.

Water sluices down Summer's back as she arches it, letting out a throaty moan that carries over the surface. Tyler's brow is furrowed, concentration in every line of his face as he fucks her.

I roll my eyes and lean against Tommy.

"Couldn't they wait until we were all back at our cabins?"

I mean, that's what *we* are planning on doing…

"And allow us to deprive them of the chance to show off that they still fuck like bunnies even if they're married?" teases Tommy.

I snort. "Please. They act like they're the only ones who know what it's like to have been hitched. I was married too, once."

And I still have the ring on my finger to prove it.

Tommy loops his arm over my shoulder, tucking me into his side. "I bet you and Clay never fucked with an audience before."

He'd lose that bet, too.

Not that I have any intention of telling Tommy about what my love life with his best friend was like, but it's true.

We were in our early twenties when Clay died. Up until the morning he left for work, never to come home to me again, we were banging two, maybe three times a day. When he needed me, I was ready, and it didn't matter where. Someone might see us? That got him even hotter because he loved the idea of everyone knowing that I was his. So though he didn't go out of his way to fuck me in front of other people like Summer and Tyler are doing right now, he wouldn't pull out, either, until he'd finished inside of me.

Despite what she implied earlier, I'm not a prude. I'm also not going to treat Tommy like Clay just to one-up Summer fucking Kaye. He's different. Sweeter. Gentler, too. Clay was so possessive, and sometimes I forget that Tommy isn't like that. He's protective, yes, but if I ended things with him tomorrow, he'd be heartbroken, but able to move on.

With Clay, it took death to rip him away, and even then I can't stop feeling like he's haunting me.

That's why, if it's up to me, I'd never talk about my time with Clay to Tommy. He's gone, and maybe it's not the healthiest response in the world, but it's easier for me to act like he never existed.

But Tommy… he made it so easy for me to give him a second chance. If he'd been the type of guy who couldn't get over my being a widow, this never would've worked. If he held a grudge that I chose Clay over him, I'd have to end it. And if he wanted me to love him and pretend that Clay meant nothing to me…

Never.

That's not Tommy Gillis, though. He's a good guy. Thoughtful, too. He hasn't moved away from my side since the second we approached the lake. Like always, he's my shoulder to lean on.

But I'm okay. Really. And when he ducks under the water, popping back up again a couple of feet away, shaking his soaked curls out and spraying me with the chilly droplets, I don't reach out to grab him closer.

Instead, I watch as all of these people I've known most of my life swim and play and have fun.

New memories, I think to myself.

Madison shrieks as Chase, maybe a little too playful, dumps water on her perfectly styled hair. She pushes the damp strands out of her face, then smacks him in the chest. He grins, grabbing her hand, pulling her close to him so he can kiss her quickly.

She melts against him, and I look away before they decide to pull a Summer and Ty and start fucking.

Group getaway, huh? Too bad Aaron didn't come. Without meaning to, it's turned into a couples' vacation, after all, with everyone pairing up.

To my left, Vee's treading water now, drifting closer to the shore. Summer calls out to her—the same time I hear Tyler's telltale grunts behind me—but Vee ignores her.

I turn slightly to see that Summer is clinging to Tyler,

the satisfied, sleepy look on her face making it obvious she got what she wanted from her husband before he did. His hand is rubbing circles on her naked back, clutching her to him as if afraid to let her go.

She's watching Vee while idly running her fingers through Tyler's hair.

I drift a few steps closer to Vee.

Tommy catches my attention. He puts his finger to his lips, eyes sparkling with mischief.

He ducks under the water again. From the ripples on the surface, he's heading toward Vee.

Vee crosses her arms over her chest with one arm. With the other, she points toward the shore. "Hey, guys? Did anyone else see—"

She goes under. It all happens so fast. Her arms go up, her body goes down, and before I know it, she's gone.

I panic. "Vee!"

Seconds later, she resurfaces, hair sticking to her face, eyes blazing with fury. Right next to her, Tommy pokes his head out of the water, keeping the rest of his body hidden as though he's kneeling in the lake.

"Gotcha," he says, laughing.

He thinks it's funny. Fuck. As I clutch my chest, willing my racing heart to slow, I'm thinking he's the only one.

Vee sputters, slapping her hands against the lake's surface, sending water everywhere. "You asshole!"

Tommy's laughter dies. Luckily, it's the only thing that does. "What's wrong?"

"What's wrong? Your fucking stunt! I'd expect that from Aaron. Not you, Tommy. What the hell?"

"I'm so sorry, Vee. I was just—"

"Dicking around. Are you serious? With Cyn right there? Did you want to remind her of how her mom died?"

Oof.

Tommy's expression is suddenly horrified. He spins around, soaked curls spraying water everywhere again as he searches for me. "Cyn, you know I didn't—"

I know.

He's so damn determined to help *me* forget what happened on the island, *he* completely forgot how fucking easy it would be to re-traumatize me.

And there's no way any of us can leave until Monday morning.

So I smile at him. It's shaky at best, probably because the rest of me is trembling, but damn it, I *smile*.

"It's okay," I lie. "But if you don't mind, I think that's enough of the lake for me tonight."

This time, not a single person tries to make me feel bad for wanting to end the night earlier than the others.

THE WALK BACK TO OUR CABINS IS A LOT MORE AWKWARD than it was when I was dreading reaching the lake. At least, then, I was the only one who was hanging back, staying quiet, holding onto Tommy's hand so that I didn't lose my nerve and turn around.

Now? I know that everyone is remembering what happened to my mom at the lake.

Tommy tried to apologize on three separate occasions. I cut him off each time. He doesn't have anything to be sorry about. He was having fun with an old friend. If anything, it's Violet who's stewing quietly as she marches ahead of us.

She has her phone out, flashlight on as she sweeps it through the trees. There are a couple of worn dirt paths that lead from the camping area to the lake. They've existed for decades, from every local mainlander who came to visit Halo Island over the years. The new owners might have renovated the actual cabins, building an honest-to-God bonfire pit instead of us all relying on some dried wood, a match, and a prayer, but they've left these old paths alone.

It's weird that Vee's searching the woods. The path is clear in front of us, and the best thing about island life is that we don't have to worry about black bears and mountain lions. Most of the wildlife here are small mammals: foxes, mice, squirrels, and skunks. If we don't bother them, they won't bother us.

But when Chase asked what Vee was looking for, she shot Tommy a dirty look, shook her head, and picked up the pace so she could get further away from the rest of us.

I didn't know what that was about. I didn't really care

that much, either. I just wanted to get back to the cabin, shower off the lake, and settle into bed with Tommy.

It's been a long, emotional day. Tommy can sense how worn out I am. Instead of offering for us to share the shower—knowing we'll do a hell of a lot more than getting clean if we do—he turns the faucet on for me, getting it to the perfect steamy temp, then heads back into the bedroom while I shower off first.

Tommy insisted, and I gratefully accepted.

He's learned that taking long, hot showers is self-care for me. I can stand beneath the spray for an hour, letting the water run down on me, and lose myself in all of the emotions I struggle with. Throw in exfoliating, shaving, washing and conditioning my long hair, and putting on lotion when I'm done and it's not unusual for me to be in the bathroom for closer to an hour and a half.

I do that tonight. Knowing he's out there, keeping me safe and protected, allows me to wash away the remnants of Halo Lake.

As soon as I'm finally done, my wet hair twisted up in one towel, another towel wrapped around my body, I move out into the bedroom and notice two very distinct things: Tommy has laid out one of my favorite, comfortable sleep shirts on the bed for me—and he's not alone.

"Summer?" I tighten my grip on my towel. "What are you doing here?"

WELCOME TO
HALO ISLAND

'til death
do we part...

EIGHT

STAY WITH ME

Her gaze goes from the amount of cleavage I have on display courtesy of the short towel all the way to the toenails I painted black to match my fingernails.

Shockingly, she keeps her judgmental comments to herself.

"I couldn't sleep," Summer tells me. "Tyler said he would just go with Vee for, like, twenty minutes and be right back. That was an hour ago."

I blink, utterly confused. "Sorry. I missed something. Where did Tyler and Vee go?"

"It's okay, love. Summer was just telling me what happened. Did you know Vee swears she saw someone in the woods?"

My heart jolts. "Um. No. I didn't."

"It's why she was so pissed at me for messing around in the water. She thought there was someone watching us when we were in the lake. Me being a boneheaded idiot, I didn't realize she was staring at the trees for a reason. I just pulled her under for fun, and when she popped up again, they were supposedly gone."

No. *No.* "No one's supposed to be on the island. Aaron backed out. It's just the seven of us, and we were all in the water."

"That's what I told her," Summer says. "She's convinced there was someone there. When we got back to the cabins, she got all worked up again. Said she couldn't go to bed until she checked to make sure her dumbass ex wasn't trying to pull a prank on us."

Oh. I get it. "She thinks Aaron changed his mind and somehow convinced Mulligan to bring him here super late. We didn't know because we were at the lake, and he must've figured out we'd be there."

Summer shrugs. "Something like that, I guess. Doesn't matter. Madi and Chase wanted to go to sleep." The way she says 'sleep' tells me that one of the cabins we booked will definitely be going empty tonight. There are six of them, perfect when we thought that Tommy and I would have one, Summer and Tyler another, then Vee, Chase, Madison, and Aaron all taking their own. But if Madison and Chase went to sleep together… "I wanted a shower. Tyler offered to go because of course he did. Always gotta be the knight in shining armor to someone." She blows out a breath of air. "Twenty minutes. That's what he said. But they're not back yet."

Okay. Knowing Vee and her Type-A personality, if

she thinks Aaron is fucking with us by hiding on the island, she won't go to bed until she's searched every inch herself. Tyler will try to talk her down if possible.

I get all that. But why is Summer in *our* cabin?

"I was just seeing if Tommy wanted to help me find my husband. Vee can look all she wants, but I'm ready to go to bed, and I'm not sleeping alone."

How nice. She doesn't want to sleep alone, so what is she trying to do? Take *my* bedmate with her.

"I'm sure they'll be back any minute now," I tell Summer. "It's almost, what? Two in the morning? Vee might be determined, but she needs sleep, too."

Summer huffs. "I'm not worried about Vee. I just want Tyler." She bats her lashes at Tommy. "Please? You know how bad my sense of direction is. If I go looking for my husband, I might end up on the other end of the island with no way to get back to the cabins."

I give her a thin-lipped smile. "The island's a circle. Eventually you'll find your way back."

"But what if there is someone out there?" she says softly. She looks imploringly up at Tommy. "What if it's not Aaron?"

It's not possible, but I know Tommy. The second she dropped her voice like that, sounding as vulnerable as she did? He'll help her.

Giving me an apologetic smile, he says, "Come with us?"

I've got a towel on, and my hair is soaked. I'm not going anywhere—and he knows it.

"I'm exhausted. I need to go to bed."

Stay with me.

I don't say the words. What's the point? If he does stay, I'm a controlling bitch who won't let him help a friend in need. If he doesn't, he'll feel guilty for refusing me. I have to let him make his own choices—

"Get your rest, love." Tommy pats the front pocket of his jeans. "I've got the key to the cabin. I'll lock the door behind me. Don't wait up. I'll be back before you know it."

—even if I think it's the wrong one.

***

CALL ME CONTRARY IF YOU WANT, BUT WHEN TOMMY SAID not to wait up? I couldn't bring myself to be a good little girl and listen.

I brushed my hair, piling it on top of my head since I'm not the biggest fan of sleeping with wet hair, and for all the amenities the new owners of Halo Island provided, a hair dryer isn't one of them. I yanked on my sleep shirt, snorting in annoyance when I noticed that my boyfriend laid out the shirt and no panties.

Ha. He must've been expecting to get laid, only for Summer to cockblock him.

I didn't bother finding a pair to shimmy on myself. Instead, I laid on the bed, legs crossed, arms crossed, waiting for Tommy to return to the cabin like he promised.

I wasn't lying before, though. I *am* exhausted. Both physically and mentally. The light in the cabin started giving me a headache. I clicked it off, then curled up on my side, promising myself I wouldn't go to sleep until Tommy was with me again.

Since I get woken up to what feels like much later to a warm, naked chest at my back and a probing finger sliding through my folds, I obviously failed on that front.

He knows the moment I go from being fast asleep to partly awake. Pressing a kiss to the side of my neck, he gathers up some of the moisture on his fingertip, then dips it inside of me.

I arch my back, shoving my pussy against his hand. He's still wearing his jeans, though his shirt must be off. The denim material scratches my ass as I take his entire finger inside of my pussy.

He must've been fingering me longer than I thought. My body is already responding to him, lubing me up so that I take him easily. That's not that unusual. Since Tommy and I started to live together, there are times he wakes up in the middle of the night with a hard-on. I gave him permission to fuck my pussy whenever he wanted, so long as he made sure I was wet and stretched out for him. If that meant using artificial lube or playing with me with his finger first, that was fine. More often than not, I wake up to him doing it, then I get to enjoy my pleasure, too.

Like now.

He knows all of my erogenous zones. Between suckling on the side of my throat and sucking my earlobe into the warmth of his mouth, I'm both aroused and half-asleep.

Mumbling softly as he fucks me with his finger, I ask, "Tommy? Did you find them?"

"Mm," he says. He's scraping my earlobe with his teeth now, sending shivers down my spine at the sensation.

I'm going to take that answer as a yes anyway. If Tyler and Vee are still lost on the island somewhere, I can't imagine Tommy giving up the search just because he's horny and needs to get laid. Especially since Summer would probably just bat her lashes at him again, using Tommy's kind heart to get her way.

"I'm glad," I say, arching into him. Fuck. That finger feels amazing, but I need *more*. I'm ready for him, and now that I have him back in my bed where he belongs, it feels like he's just teasing me by not pulling his fingers out and shoving his cock in. Reaching behind me, I clutch his thigh through his jeans. "I missed you."

He releases my earlobe, using the edge of his teeth to trail the back of my neck instead.

I start to pant a little. "Stop teasing me," I say.

Warm breath washes over me as he chuckles huskily.

Fucking Tommy. There are times when he treats me like a pillow princess, doing everything he can to make sure I come first. Then there are those nights when he can't keep himself from fucking me, whether I'm awake or not. But, when I least expect it, his teasing takes on almost a punishing edge, making me wait for him like he waited so long for me to find my way back into his arms.

I'm here now. I need him, and I whisper a plea. "I *need* you."

That usually does the trick. This time is no different. As soon as he says that, he pulls his finger out. Still stroking me, circling my clit, driving me wild with his possessive touch, the bed dips, and I hear his jeans rustle.

Suddenly, something much thicker is prodding my entrance. I'm so ready for him that he slips through the moisture gathered there. He grumbles, I suck in a breath, and I don't know what he's doing back there, but he shoves into me with one firm stroke.

I groan.

God, maybe it's this position, or maybe he needed to use two fingers to stretch me out, because I'm suddenly super full.

I arch my back, getting comfortable as he seats himself inside of me. But when I try to move with him, he stills me by laying his hand on my hip before sliding it up, cupping my tit. He tucks his other arm beneath me, grabbing the other one.

"Like this," he whispers. "Let me hold you."

His voice sounds strange. Lower than normal. Because it's so late and he hasn't gone to bed yet? That happens to me sometimes. I use my voice too much that it becomes raspy and unfamiliar, just like Tommy's.

My body recognizes his, though. His touch makes it sing, and with a tit in each palm, caging me against him with his arms around me and his cock buried to the hilt inside of me, it's a fucking symphony of sensation.

He's tweaking my nipples, sending jolts of pleasure running through me. As he slowly starts to move his hips, taking leisurely thrusts that he punctuates with another tug on my tits, I throw my head back against him and moan.

It's been a long day. I wouldn't mind him taking his time, worshiping my body like he loves to do, but when his fucking takes on urgency, like he's racing a clock somewhere, I'm grateful. A quickie and then a couple of more hours' sleep sounds perfect, and Tommy seems to be on the same page.

He knows me so well. My sounds change, becoming quicker, my moans louder the closer I get to climaxing. Right when I'm on the verge, he flicks my clit, and the pressure building up inside of me explodes. I shriek, and Tommy bites down on my shoulder.

Now that I've come, he fucks me like, if he doesn't finish and *now*, he might just explode next.

I let him. I lay there and take it, and when he bucks up inside of me, filling me with his come, I stroke his thigh possessively even as my eyes begin to close again.

He holds me closer, whispering softly against my skin. "Love you, baby."

That shows just how boneless and relaxed the orgasm he gave me just made me. I don't even tense up or react when he uses Clay's pet name for me.

I just stay connected to him, letting him thrust gently

into me as I pillow my head on my hands and drift back to unconsciousness.

———

I wake up to a little tenderness down below and my thighs sticking together.

Ah, crap. I'm usually so much better at remembering to get up, pee, and tidy up after sex. I was prone to getting UTIs when I first started sleeping with Tommy as a teen, and after the third one, my mother flat-out asked if we were sexually active. We were fifteen, young and stupid, and extremely lucky that we never had a pregnancy scare since, even then, I knew I never wanted to have kids.

My mom was great. No judgment from her, though she helped me get on birth control almost immediately. I got the safe sex lecture, too—and a box of condoms that we tried our best to remember to use—plus some advice to keep the UTIs from coming back.

The amount of come slicking my legs closed tells me that Tommy didn't bother grabbing one of the condoms he promised he packed in his duffel bag. It happens. Sometimes he's so eager to get inside of me, we're already fucking before it hits me that he's bareback. I've never gone off birth control, though I rely on an IUD now, plus we're exclusive, so it doesn't really bother me when he forgets to wrap up as long as I remember to clean up when we're done.

I didn't last night. There was something about how he fucked me in the dark of the cabin, an unfamiliar place, purposely thrusting up into me from behind. I didn't see his face. He barely spoke, except for panting my name and grunting as he came. In the haze that came from being half awake as he fucked me, I could fantasize that he was anyone.

My stomach goes uneasy as I remember the dreams that followed me after he banged me to sleep.

Clay. Once Tommy got me off, then came inside of me, he refused to let his cock slips out. I could sense how much he needed the connection, and the euphoria that slammed into me when he plucked my clit and I screamed faded so quickly, I drifted back into unconsciousness while warming his cock.

Obviously, he pulled away at some point in the night. Now he's sleeping next to me, deliciously shirtless, though he has his jeans on. The fly's open, zipper down, his dick tucked inside of his pants. One arm is thrown over his face, shielding him against the sunlight streaming in through the window.

For a moment, I think about reaching into his pants and pulling him out. He banged some of my anxiousness out of me last night, and I've got the evidence of our mutual enjoyment still between my thighs. I'm in a much better mood today. Assuming he freshened up himself since he's redressed, I kind of want to take care of his morning wood with my mouth.

Morning sex sounds good, too. I mean. I need to

shower again anyway. Why not wait until we both get good and sweaty? And if I like the idea of waking up our cabin neighbors with the inevitable scream I'll let out? Can't help it. I'm a screamer, and when I have a partner who knows how to work my body like it belongs to him, I'm not shy about letting others know that.

Just before I scoot closer to him, it's another scream that rents through the air. An unholy scream, so high-pitched and frantic, I freeze in place.

Did I hear that?

It rings out again, full of agony, and I know I didn't imagine it.

Tommy didn't rouse at the first scream. With the second? He jerks awake, slapping himself in the face. Pulling his body into a sitting position, he rubs his forehead, looking for me.

"Cyn?" He frowns. "What's going on?"

I have no fucking clue.

"I heard a scream. Two of them. It came from outside."

"Yeah. That's what I thought I heard, too. Kinda thought it was a dream, but… Wait." There's a night-stand on each side of the bed. Tommy's phone and the key to our cabin are sitting on top of his. He grabs the phone, tilting it to see the time. "It's almost ten."

Shit. We slept in that late? I mean, I know we didn't get back to the cabin until almost one. Then Vee and Tyler went searching for some bogeyman she thought she saw, followed by Summer and Tommy going searching for *them*. I don't know how late it was when Tommy came back and we had sex before falling asleep together.

So it's not as early as I thought. But that doesn't change anything.

Who's screaming?

I look at Tommy. He starts to climb out of the bed.

No longer in the mood for morning sex, I slide out of my side.

Tommy doesn't stop to grab a shirt. All I have on is my sleep shirt, but he's almost at the door. There's no time for me to throw on clothes. I just pad behind him, peeking around Tommy's lean back after he pushes the cabin door out.

Summer. Of course it has to be Summer.

She's standing with Tyler and Chase. Chase is pacing a few feet away from the married couple, and Tyler has his arms wrapped around his wife. She's shaking her head back and forth, looking like she's trying to claw her way out of Tyler's embrace.

Tommy dashes down the handful of stairs that lead to our porch.

I step out onto the porch itself, hovering there as Summer's head turns, finding our cabin.

"We have to tell Tommy," she yells at Tyler, shoving him away.

The big man releases her. Within seconds, she's fleeing toward my boyfriend, flinging her arms around him.

Jealousy rips through me, but when I see the tracks of tears running down Summer's cheeks, I go cold.

Screaming, I think. She was screaming.

Wait. Where's Madison? Where's V—

"It's Vee… Tommy, it's *Vee*."

He pats the back of her head while Tyler stays where he was, expression flat though his dark brown eyes seem even darker. Like they're all pupil.

Like he's inwardly panicking.

Chase is still pacing, biting down on his bottom lip, his hands in his pockets.

Everyone is dressed but Tommy and me. They all look like they've been through the wringer, too, and whatever Summer's about to say, I suddenly don't want to hear it.

But she can't find the words. Clinging to Tommy, openly sobbing now, the sounds she's making are indecipherable.

I inch my bare feet down the steps, moving past them so that I can address Tyler.

Of the group, he's the one I've spent the least amount of time with alone since I moved back to Gullhaven. I know that's because—as much as Summer still has a thing for my boyfriend—his wife is careful to keep me away from her husband. It is what it is, but I've never had a problem with Tyler. In my opinion, I question his taste since he always comes crawling back to Summer when she shakes her tits and crooks her finger, but other than that, he's a simple kind of guy who doesn't like to fuck around.

"Ty?" I ask, knowing that I don't want to hear his answer—but accepting that I *have* to. "What happened to Vee?"

He gulps, hands hanging at his side helplessly. "She's fucking dead, Cyn. I found her. She's *dead*."

What?

WELCOME TO
HALO ISLAND
'til death
do we part...

NINE
ACCIDENT

Tommy did everything but lock me in the cabin to try to convince me I didn't need to see this. I disagreed. Vee… She's my friend.

Was my friend.

I owed it to her. To be there with everyone else instead of letting Tommy coddle me, leaving me behind… I had to go. Madison couldn't bring herself to see Vee like that, but Summer, Chase, Tyler, and Tommy were all going to check out the scene and figure out what our next move was going to be. Once Madison said she'd be okay if we left her behind, Tommy and I hurriedly got dressed. As soon as we were ready, Tyler led us to the ravine where Vee fell.

I'll admit, I experienced the teeniest, tiniest twinge of relief when I learned that she didn't drown, but somehow fell about twenty or so feet in the ravine that helps feed Halo Lake.

I don't know how it happened. Everyone who's ever spent time on the island knows about the ravine—and to avoid it. It's the only break in the actual 'halo', spanning about thirty feet across. Because there are other ways to cross the island, no one's ever bothered building a bridge to span it. Technically, we can climb down it, too, since it's on a slant with rocky handholds for the way back up, though I definitely wouldn't recommend it.

Is that what happened? Did Vee decide she wanted to cross it and thought that would be easier than following the ravine to the lake and cutting back that way?

There's no way to know. All we have is her broken body at the bottom of the ravine, and that's not answering any questions for us, is it?

She's wearing the same clothes she had on the night before. That's the only thing I take in when I tiptoe to the edge of the ravine and peek down. She's wearing the same clothes... Vee doesn't sleep in her clothes. I remember that from high school sleepovers, and from things Aaron let slip while they were dating. Vee favors silky pajama sets, and even if she didn't bring any, she would've changed before heading out again.

But she didn't. Does that mean she never returned to her cabin?

She had to have, though. Right? I asked Tommy last night... he and Summer found the other two and everyone turned in to their respective cabins.

Right?

Tommy runs his fingers through his curls. He

managed to peer down into the ravine longer than both Summer and me. Tyler didn't even approach the edge again. I guess he's already seen everything he needed to.

Chase is the one who lingers the longest. Even after Tommy gulps, swiping his hand over his face, looking lost and angry and helpless… even after he wraps me up in his arms and I realize I'm crying silent tears, Chase still stares down at Vee.

His back snaps straight. Careful not to lose his footing and join Vee on the ground, he turns, hands folded behind him.

Chase's hazel eyes lock on Tyler. "Okay. Start from the beginning again, Ty. What happened?"

"Are you fucking serious, Chase?" A touch of hysteria tinges Summer's voice. "You don't think Tyler has anything to do with what happened to Vee, do you?"

"Of course not." Chase's tone is soothing. "It's obviously a terrible accident. But we need to have our stories straight—"

"Straight?" she echoes, her voice almost as high-pitched as her earlier scream. "Like we're *lying*?"

"No, no. Summer. Please. I know this is hard, but we have to stay calm—"

"How are we supposed to do that?" Tommy asks, his voice flat. "Vee is dead—"

Dead. God. The word is so fucking final. *Dead.*

There's no coming back. One wrong step and any of us could've been gone. Vee grew up on Halo Island like we all did. She never would've gone near the ravine.

Unlike Summer, her sense of direction is excellent. She wouldn't have fallen.

But she *must* have.

Chase exhales. "I know. I *saw*. But we need to know what happened. When we can eventually contact the cops—"

My stomach lurches.

Summer moans.

Right. *Cops*. We're going to have to tell them. I mean, we can't leave Vee here forever. For one thing, Mulligan will notice if we road out to the island with seven guests but leave with six. For another, she needs to be returned to her family.

Oh, God. We're going to have to explain to her *family…*

Chase surges on. "The cops will see that it's an accident. But I'm a lawyer, guys. You know that. Think. We know none of us did this to our friend. *We* know. The cops don't. We have to make sure we know what we're going to tell them. We're in this together. Tommy? Ty? You understand, don't you, Cyn? Summer… we have to know what happened. I'm not picking on Tyler. I'm just asking because he found her."

"Yeah. I did." A hollow laugh escapes him. "Threw up over there," he adds, gesturing closer to the edge of the ravine. "Shit. If I hadn't stopped to take a piss, I don't even know I would've even noticed her down there."

Tommy's laugh is just as hollow. "Fucking hell, Ty. You wanted to piss in the ravine? What are you, twelve?"

"It's just a thing I did when I was a kid. Be glad I wanted to see my piss arc into the hole otherwise we'd still be looking for Vee."

"What were you doing out here anyway?" I ask, wiping my tears away with the back of my hand. Focus, Cyn. Try to figure this shit out. "You've got a toilet back at your cabin."

Through her puffy eyes, Summer glares at me. "Weren't you listening before when he was trying to explain? We went to wake up Vee this morning to see if she wanted to have breakfast with us. She was missing. Probably gone to find that mysterious man of hers again. Tyler went to see if he could track her down and… and…"

And he did.

I shake my head. "Why would she do that? Didn't you guys clear the island last night?"

After all, they were gone for so long, I could've sworn they *had* to have.

But Tyler shakes his head. "We gave up searching after a while. I headed back to my cabin. Vee went in hers. Summer was gone—"

"Yeah." She gestures at Tommy. "Because we were looking for you two."

"I know. I stayed up until Tommy and Summer came back. Tommy went to check on Cyn, and me and Summer went to sleep. We had no idea that Vee must've gone back out after that until I saw her down there this morning. She had to have fallen. I just… are we sure she's dead?" I can hear the hope in his voice. "I didn't go down there. I didn't check. Maybe she just broke her leg and… and she's sleeping now. Right? It could happen."

Poor Tyler. He'd never been the brightest bulb in the bunch, but if he saw the same twisted body I did, he knows she's gone. For fuck's sake, she's on her back, but her head is turned away, face hidden. That's a broken neck if I ever saw one.

Summer glares at him through her own tears. "Please. Don't be a fucking idiot, Tyler. She's dead. She fell… what if someone did it to her? Shit. What if it's not an accident at all?"

What? No. It *has* to be.

The others seem to agree, but Summer turns her despair on Chase. "You were fucking Vee two months ago," she snaps. "Maybe you did it. Where were you last night anyway?"

If she turned on me like that, I'd lose it. But Chase… he just keeps calm. "I know you want to protect Tyler, but my fling with Vee doesn't mean I… what? Pushed her?"

"Maybe."

Tommy gentles his voice. "Summer…"

She ignores him. "Does Chase have an alibi? I know you were pushing Vee to be exclusive, but after everything that happened with Aaron, she blew you off. That screams motive to me."

I know Summer's gone too far this time when Chase's expression hardens. "Actually, I do have an alibi. If you don't believe me, ask Madi. It would've been kind of hard for me to sneak out and kill Vee when I was fucking her all night. C'mon, Sum. She's your best friend. You know how insatiable she is. Once she had my dick in that vice of a pussy she's got, you think she was letting me go anywhere?"

Summer's gaze lands on me. "Okay. Cyn's the only killer we have here. Maybe she did it."

I startle, gaping at Summer as it dawns on me what she just said. "Excuse me? What the fuck?"

"You heard me." She's more than a little hysterical now, but if she's going to accuse me of something so heinous… "Death follows you around, doesn't it? Your mom died and, whoops, you're the one who found her. Clay disappeared, no body, just blood, and in a couple of years, you'll get all his money. I don't know why you targeted Vee, but she's gone. Who's next? Me? Tommy?"

I knew it. I fucking knew she believed I had something to do with Clay's death. As if I would. As if I didn't pray every goddamn night that my husband would return to me.

I'm so shocked by her baseless accusation that I just continue to stare at her.

As always, Tommy rides to my rescue. "Stop it, Summer. Just stop it. You know Cyn has nothing to do with any of that. Besides, Vee was already in her cabin when we went back. The light was on. You even pointed it out. If she left after that, I was already in bed with Cyn."

"Of course you'd say that—"

"We fucked when he got back." I gesture at my thighs. "I'm still covered in come if you want to check. If you need proof that damn bad."

Tommy shields his mouth with his hand, hiding his sudden inappropriate smile.

Summer's expression turns murderous.

I raise my eyebrows at her. "How do we know *you* didn't do it?"

Tyler pales. "That's not funny, Cyn."

Yeah? Well, neither was his wife implying I had anything to do with the tragedies in my own life.

Chase sighs. "Okay. Enough. None of us did it. And since nobody ran into some phantom on the island last night, we're going to call this what it is: a terrible fucking accident. Now, that settled, we have to figure out what we're going to do next…"

I WISH WE HAD A BETTER ANSWER FOR THAT.

Spoiler alert: we don't.

It all comes down to the inexplicable reality that we're trapped on an island, fifteen miles from shore, with the corpse of one of our closest friends. To make it worse, we had to leave her there. Even if we could figure out how to scale the ravine, then drag her body back up,

Chase's lawyer instincts are in overdrive. He insists we have to preserve the scene. An accident it may be, but we need everything to look exactly the way it was for when we can finally contact the police.

That won't be until Monday morning. When the owners touted the new and improved Halo Island as a place to visit when you want to unplug and unwind, they weren't kidding. We can't contact the real world. If we'd expected anything like this, maybe a sat phone would've done the job, but our regular cells are worthless.

Obviously, Vee's death puts a damper on the rest of the getaway. Summer never said another word after I shut her down so crudely, and Tyler agreed to everything Chase insisted on just so he could get away from the ravine again.

We're all headed home on the ferry on Monday. Chase offers to come back with the cops to show them where Vee is, but until then, he suggests we all return to our cabins, try to enjoy the rest of our weekend, and deal with the real world when we can.

The five of us are a somber group as we return to the row of cabins. Chase heads into the one he shared with Madison last night, presumably to fill her in on what we all discussed. Summer and Tyler head toward theirs.

Tommy takes my hand and guides me to ours.

Once the cabin door is closed behind us and it's just Tommy and me alone again, I shudder out a breath as he releases me.

Tommy squeezes my shoulder in passing as I move further into the front room. "You okay, Cyn?"

Honestly? "Just trying to make sense of the bizarro world we're living in."

"Huh?"

"Think about it. Who would've thought we'd all listen to anything *Chase Whitmore* had to say?"

And Vee's gone. Only in a bizarro world could we find our friend dead and pretend we're going to enjoy the rest of our getaway while we hope no predators decide to take a chomp out of her.

I swallow a sob. Tommy's been eyeing me like he expects me to crack any second now. I'm stronger than that. I've survived so much more than a woman should've.

I can do this.

Does he agree? He bites the corner of his mouth, then exhales. "That's his job. He's trying to keep us all out of trouble."

"He's trying to cover his own ass," I mutter.

Tommy allows that. "Chase has his issues. But he's a good lawyer. No one's going to blame us for an accident."

I hope not.

Sinking down on the bed, I rub my forehead.

Tommy drops down into a crouch in front of me. "I mean it, love. Tell me. Are you okay? 'Cause if you'd rather I swim all the way back to Gullhaven and tell Mulligan we need the ferry now, I'll do it. Say the word."

I choke on a strangled laugh. "There's sharks in the water."

"Don't care."

"It's fifteen miles, Tommy!"

He puffs out his chest. "That's nothing. You want me to do it, I will."

I shake my head. How does he do that? How does he make the heavy cloud of grief dissipate just enough to let the sunshine in?

"It's okay. *I'm* okay."

His worried eyes search my face. "Really?"

I blow out a rush of air through my nose. "No. Not even a little. A girl I've known since I was five is dead. She slipped and fell. That could've been any of us." I lay my hands on his shoulders. "It could've been *you.*"

He covers my hands with his. "Nothing's going to happen to me."

I really hope so. Speaking around the lump in my throat, I whisper, "I've lost too many people in my life already. I can't do it again."

Tommy firms his features. "I waited too long for a second chance with you, Cyn. Believe me. It's going to take a lot more than a freak accident to keep me from you."

I really fucking hope so—but I know better.

Clay used to say the same exact things to me, and I lost him anyway.

Damn it. I can't say goodbye to anyone else, but I

can't help but think that Halo Island isn't done with me just yet.

And there are plenty more people I *can* lose.

WELCOME TO
HALO ISLAND

'til death
do we part...

TEN
SCREAM

I can't sleep. Not really.

Damn it.

The first few months after Clay disappeared on me, my therapist hooked me up with a psychiatrist. Dr. Lucas couldn't prescribe me antidepressants or sleeping pills, but Dr. Hogel could. I guzzled them suckers like they were candy because I needed the break from reality, but once I decided I had to move on, I stopped refilling the prescription.

What I wouldn't give to have one of them now… to knock back a pill or two, conk out, and wake up to discover it was time for us to get the hell off of Halo Island.

I don't know if I would've fallen asleep at all if it wasn't for the protective way that Tommy held me, stroking my hair, murmuring softly to me so that I was able to relax just enough to sleep fitfully for a little while.

His side of the bed is empty now. I think that's what woke me up. When I couldn't sense him next to me any longer, my restless sleep became even uneasier until I woke up on my back, staring up at the ceiling.

My hand roves over the rough sheet. My first instinct was that he must've gotten up to use the bathroom. I don't think that's right. The sheets are cool, as though he's been missing for a while, and I don't see the slight yellow light seeping from under the bathroom door that shows he's in there.

I lift up on my elbows. "Tommy?"

No answer.

My heart skips a beat.

"Tommy?" A little louder this time. A little more urgent. "You here?"

I don't think he is.

My phone is on the nightstand on my side of the bed. I grab it, wincing at the bright light of the screen, then the symbol that shows there is no signal on the island. No matter how much I hope that my phone will suddenly work and we can call back to Gullhaven, it still hasn't happened yet. Tommy regretfully assures me it won't, but I keep checking anyway.

Still no service, and the clock tells me that it's only a couple of minutes past midnight.

I slept for about two hours, I guess. Not as bad as I thought, but now that I'm inwardly freaking out over Tommy being missing, there's no way in hell I can go back to sleep until I know where he is.

Using my flashlight, I tiptoe through all of the rooms of the cabin. Just like I thought, he's not here. The back door is locked, too, and when I check the front door, I see that that one *isn't*.

It was when we decided to lie down. I watched Tommy turn it himself. Did he leave? Where did he go?

Visions of Vee's broken body flash across my mind. I swallow roughly, eager to push them back. No dice. Instead, Vee's replaced by Tommy. His deep blue eyes wide and staring, his body crumpled on the ground.

My hand shakes. What if something happened to him?

I move toward the window.

My heart beats triple-time when I see a shadowy figure walking down one of the other porches to a different cabin.

I can't see who they are. Silhouetted against the faint moonlight, they seem to be dressed all in black. A hooded sweatshirt. Dark pants. A shadow falls in front of their face so I can't make out any details there. The height makes me think 'male', but willowy Madison is almost as tall as Tommy, so that doesn't really help.

Who is that?

Then, a better question: whose *cabin* is that?

Mine and Tommy's is at the end. Chase's is next, but he spent last night with Madison. He's probably been with her since we left Vee at the ravine, so it's empty—and that's not the one I just saw the shadowy figure step out of.

The next one is Vee's. The one after that is also empty because it was meant for Aaron. But the fifth one…

That's Summer and Tyler's cabin.

Weird. If that's Tyler… what is he doing? But Tyler is bulkier than the figure I saw leaving the cabin. So, who else could it be?

And why did they stop at the end, turning directly to look at the last cabin in the row, almost like they were searching for *me*?

I don't know, but I'm already super jumpy after waking up and seeing that Tommy is gone. Inching away from the window, I turn my back on it. Another peek to make sure the door is locked, and I tiptoe all the way back to the second room.

But I don't go to sleep. I can't. I sit up in bed, the light on, until I hear the door unlocking.

My heart leaps up to my throat. Too late, it hits me that I should've grabbed a weapon from the kitchen. A knife, maybe, or one of the heavy pans provided so we can cook. I'm utterly defenseless—

—and Tommy startles when he sees I'm sitting up against the headboard, watching the entry to the bedroom with wide, terrified eyes.

"Cyn?"

I shudder out a breath. "*Tommy.*"

It's Tommy.

He's wearing his jeans and the same blue hoodie he always has on when he's not at work and it's too chilly for just a regular t-shirt. From a distance, though, if he had the hood up… it could look black. He could've been the shadowy figure I saw out there…

I swallow roughly. "Where were you?"

"Me? Oh. Couldn't sleep. I went out for some fresh air and caught Chase outside, smoking a cigarette. He told us all he stopped, but with the stress of Vee… he needed a hit, I guess. Madison wouldn't let him smoke inside so he was on the porch. Once he was done, we took a walk to check on Vee." He shows me the phone in his hand. "Good thing I had this for the flashlight. We had to scare a couple of predators away." His face closes off for a moment. "It was gnarly. I'm glad you didn't have to see that. I tell ya, I'll be happy when it's Monday and we can get off the island. Won't you?"

I nod, still trying to imagine if Tommy could've been the person I saw. But it couldn't have been. He was with Chase…

"And Chase is in his cabin? No more accidents?"

Tommy's expression turns concerned. "Cyn, love? You okay? You're looking at me like you saw a ghost or something."

I don't know what I saw.

I shake my head. "Yeah. Sorry. I couldn't sleep, either."

I don't think I'll be able to sleep again until we're off of Halo Island again.

Surprisingly, I do.

That's exhaustion for you. My mind was wired, my body tired, and one of them had to give out. After an hour of lying next to Tommy, relieved at least that he was safe and able to rest, I finally did fall asleep.

When we don't wake up the next morning to a scream, I'm so fucking relieved, you have no idea. Vee's death is a tragedy, but it was an accident. Now we just have to make it until tomorrow morning before Mulligan returns and we can alert the authorities about it. But that's all it was. An accident.

Right?

I get to think that for most of the day. Following yesterday's routine, Tommy and I linger in our cabin. I make breakfast of pancakes and bacon while he's slumbering peacefully. I'm careful not to look out the window again in case I see something that's not there, all while pretending that everything is okay.

After we eat, I shower. Get dressed. I ignore Tommy's obvious disappointment that I didn't invite him into the shower with me or decide to spend the day in bed with him. Instead, I curl up on the couch in the front room and turn on the DVD player that came standard in each cabin. There's no cable or internet, so no streaming, but our room has six hand-picked DVDs, all for the upcoming Halloween holiday.

I pass on *Nightmare on Elm Street*, *Friday the 13th*, and *Halloween*, the classic itself. I almost put on *Scream*, but the opening sequence with a terrorized blonde and her high school sweetheart in the varsity jacket fucks me up. It reminds me too much of me and, well, both Tommy and Clay. I was a nobody at Gullhaven High who ended up dating both the quarterback of the football team (plus the first baseman of the baseball team) before I traded him in for the star kicker with the football scholarship out of state. Varsity jackets are still Madison's kryptonite, but I had to admit that I had a thing for them, too.

I'm twenty-seven now. A widow. I lost one of my high school boyfriends. I don't want to imagine losing the other.

That left *Nightmare Before Christmas* and *Hocus Pocus*. And as much as I grew up on the cult classics and love them both, I decided to turn on my three favorite witches.

Tommy joins me at that part when Max is lighting the black flame candle, bringing the witches back to life for one night all because he's a virgin with no impulse control.

I nod at the screen as Tommy sits on the couch, tugging me so that I'm sitting right next to him. Echoing my thought, I say, "A virgin with no impulse control. Reminds me of someone I used to know."

"Hey. You were also a virgin when we got together," he teases.

"But I had impulse control."

Back then, anyway.

"Don't I know it. You were the one who made me

wait a year before I could even put my hands in your pants."

I smirk, snuggling up against him. "It was worth it, wasn't it?"

"Oh, yeah. Believe me, Cyn. There isn't anything I won't do to keep that pussy as mine."

"Just my pussy? My tits might not be that big, but my ass is pretty nice. Plus, I can cook."

Tommy kisses my temple. "Okay. I'll keep you for your food, your ass, and your pussy. Deal?"

I shove him away from me. "You're such a fucking charmer, Tommy."

"I try," he laughs. "I try."

The mood is a lot more relaxed following that. After *Hocus Pocus* ends, I get up and make us a couple of sandwiches so that we can settle in to watch *Nightmare Before Christmas* together. I'd forgotten that Leah, Tommy's younger sister, was a huge fangirl of the film during her teen years. Leah's twenty-three now—the oldest of his siblings after Tommy—and she just had a baby in June.

Between Tommy singing along with Jack Skellington and the two of us discussing what baby Cameron is going to be for Halloween, I could almost forget that we were just waiting out the clock until we could leave the island.

The world goes on. I forget that sometimes. My life is ruled around two dates: May 15th, when my mother died, and October 28th, when I learned that Clay had disappeared. I shut down around them, mourning by myself even when I have Tommy right by my side, then exist in a world without Caroline Preston and Clayton Rivers as best I can for the months in between the next reminder.

But as the movie comes to an end, with the reminder that Jack and Sally were simply meant to be, I press a kiss to the edge of Tommy's scruff-covered jaw. *Simply meant to be…* like us?

Maybe.

If anything, I'm content at the moment. I'm not thinking about how hard Clay's anniversary is going to be come tomorrow. I'm forcing myself not to think about Vee's body being ravaged by the wildlife on the island because Chase convinced us to leave her there. I'm just enjoying this moment with Tommy, and when he suggests we give *Scream* a try next, I'm all for it—

And that's when another scream rents through our cabin, and I know in an instant that I won't be content again for a long, long time.

WELCOME TO
HALO ISLAND
'til death
do we part...

ELEVEN

KILLER

Madison is the screamer, but that's only because Summer went temporarily mute when she walked into her cabin and discovered her husband.

Because Tyler is dead.

He's dead.

He's dead, dead, *dead*…

I should've stayed outside. Looking down on Vee from the top of the ravine was one thing. That upset me, but it didn't bother me; not like it made poor Tyler puke. But there's a difference between seeing a broken body twenty feet away and standing maybe three feet away from the mess that used to be Tyler Kaye's chest.

I don't know how many times he was stabbed. Once I saw the blood, the gore, the torn-up skin and tissue that covered the blanket and sheets on the bed beneath him, I covered my mouth with my hand and hightailed it back outside where Summer was clinging to Madison.

Madison was murmuring that it'll be okay, everything will be okay, while Summer sobbed. She'd broken her stunned quiet with a howl while we were inside, almost as though it finally hit her that that hunk of blond meat was her husband, and the way she wailed was one of the reasons I followed Tommy inside with Chase.

I couldn't stay, though. I'm a horror buff, but that… it's *real*. It's not like the movies. You can smell the blood, the sickening sweetness of death, the shit he expelled when he died… the room was rancid. Rank. There was so much blood. I mentally compare it to the crime scene photos I saw of Clay's car.

That was a lot.

This is *more*.

Chase and Tommy stood over Tyler as I left, hushed murmurs passing between them about what we should do next. I'm assuming part of their decision was leaving the body alone, just like we did with Vee, because they come outside almost immediately, locking the door behind them.

If Summer notices, she doesn't say anything. She just gulps a couple of deep breaths, trying to get herself under control. She has an audience now, and if that's unkind after I saw what happened to Tyler, the way she turns her tears off as quickly as she does makes me not regret my thought.

At least, unlike Summer, I keep it to myself.

Chase waits for her to finish composing herself. What happens next is nothing less than a cross-examination, and if I liked Summer a little more, I'd feel bad for the way that Chase is going all lawyer on her so soon.

Not that I blame him. Another one of us is dead, and while it was pure luck that Tyler stumbled upon Vee's body after she fell, why the hell did it take until the afternoon for Summer to realize that her husband was lying dead in their bed?

None of us are pros, though Chase likes to think he is. We can't say for sure when Tyler died, but since he's already in rigor mortis and the spilled blood itself has started to oxidize, he's been dead for a while.

So why did Summer only *just* find him?

"That's easy. Because I didn't sleep with him last night. I only just went back to our cabin now to change and see what he was up to because I was bored. Okay?"

"If you weren't with Tyler, where did you sleep?" asks Chase.

"I slept in the vacant one next to yours," she says, tilting her chin up in defiance. "Tyler was tossing and turning 'cause of everything that happened. I just wanted to sleep, and since Aaron's not here, I took his bed."

She's lying. To be fair, if Summer's not being a total bitch to me, most of the time I expect whatever she says to be a lie. Like when she boasts about how Tyler loves her, or that she's loyal when even Vee let slip that Summer gets some on the side whenever she's bored, or that we're the bestest of best childhood friends when she'd happily throw me to the wolves if given the chance.

This is different, though. She's lying about last night. Not where she slept, because I'm pretty sure Summer's not the type of chick to make her bed up in the morning. If she was in Aaron's assigned cabin, there would be evidence of that. But why was she there? Because after the way she came to *my* cabin the night before, so desperate to go to bed with Tyler that she needed Tommy to help find her husband, I can't imagine she chose to sleep alone.

No. Something's off.

Something's not right.

I remember her reaction when I suggested she might've been involved in Vee's accident. I'd been fucking with her because, let's face it, she's Summer fucking Kaye, but I didn't honestly believe she had anything to do with the fall.

But now that Tyler's been *murdered*…

"Convenient alibi," I murmur, my voice soft though everyone gathered can definitely hear me. "You leave your husband alone just in time for him to be stabbed to death."

Summer lifts her hand as if she's going to slap me. I don't flinch. I'm not afraid of her, and she sees something in my face that has her thinking better of following through with her strike.

Shaking her hair out, her voice trembling in a combination of fury and grief, she says, "He was sleeping fitfully when I left. I even complained to Tommy and Chase when I saw them talking on the porch. And the snoring… the snoring…" Summer's voice trails off, as if realizing that despite her bitching, she'll never hear Tyler snore again. Her voice breaks, then drops. "You could hear it through the window. He was alive when I swapped cabins."

"That's right," Tommy says, confirming Summer's story. Through the sudden sheen of tears in her eyes, she gives him a thankful—and almost besotted—look. "After I talked to Chase, I poked my head in on Tyler when I heard the snoring stop. I thought he was awake, but he was tossing and turning, just like Sum said. She didn't do it."

"See? I told you—"

Madison gasps, cutting Summer off. "So you were the last one to see Tyler alive."

"What? Tommy?" Forgetting my own suspicions from last night—because, for my sanity, I *have* to—I scoff. "Are you saying that *Tommy* killed Tyler?"

Madison doesn't back down, though she does take a sidestep closer to Chase. Not Summer, I notice. *Chase.* Like he's going to protect her from *me*? Please. "I'm just saying that Tommy was the last one who saw Tyler alive. Isn't that how it works?" She glances up at Chase. "You're a lawyer. Don't the cops always suspect whoever saw the victim last? Like with Cyn and her mom?"

It takes everything I have not to react to Madison's comment. Of course. Of fucking course. One of our own has been murdered—maybe even *two*—and this dumb bitch wants to bring up my mom again.

Tommy lays his hand on my arm. "I didn't kill Tyler," he says.

"You could've," insisted Madison, all while Summer holds her tongue. It's so unlike her, I have to wonder if she has her own suspicions—and Madison is the one to voice them. "We all know you have that knife."

That's right. How could I have forgotten? A gift from his dad right before we came to Halo Island for that fateful seniors' weekend, Tommy always keeps it in his right hand back pocket.

As if proving my point, he dips his hand into that exact pocket, removing his switchblade. It's folded, and with a press of the button on the side, the knife springs open. It's about five inches long from tip to hilt, and while it could do some pretty wicked damage, it's absolutely pristine.

Does that mean he couldn't have stabbed Tyler and cleaned it off? No. I don't know what he did in the bathroom last night when he said he had to pee and changed from his daytime clothes to a pair of sweats and a t-shirt to sleep in. But, holy hell… this is *Tommy*. He couldn't have killed Tyler.

Summer didn't.

Madison was with Chase, so they couldn't have.

Vee's dead.

And I know *I* didn't do it.

So what now?

I rub my forehead, trying to make sense of this. Around me, Summer chides Madison for even suggesting Tommy would ever hurt one of us. Too little, too late, in my opinion, but I hear him murmur his appreciation for trusting him. Chase is already in lawyer mode, trying to keep everyone as calm as humanly possible. Like with Vee, he doesn't want us to touch anything, and I get that.

I also think that's the least of our concerns right now.

Vee. It all started with Violet Lee's death. But if hers was an accident, what the hell happened to Tyler?

Could he have stabbed himself? Despite the fact that Summer insists there wasn't any knife left near the bed, the scene makes it pretty fucking clear what happened: Tyler was asleep when he was stabbed for the first time. He flailed, knocking shit off the nightstand, but he was already dead; he just didn't know it yet. The added stab wounds were for insurance—or to send a message.

Vee…

I think back to the night at the lake. About how she was so adamant that she saw a stranger in the trees that she had to go searching for him.

Did she find him?

What about Tyler? He found Vee's body, and was also the only one of us who took her seriously. What did she tell him? What did he know?

Is that why he's dead now?

Who killed him?

We all have an alibi. It can't be any of us who did it — and that means only one thing.

And since no one else is saying it, I do.

"Guys, I don't think we're alone on the island anymore."

No one wants to believe we have some psycho killer on Halo Island with us barely a week before Halloween. It sounds crazy, but after the initial denial dies down, we have to accept the obvious: if we didn't kill Tyler and he didn't stab himself to death, someone else must've done it.

It all goes back to the lake. Vee thought she saw someone and most of us thought she was full of it. The ferry brought seven of us over. No other ferry will stop here because they're risking a hell of a fine. Cottonwood Harbor is small. Word would get back if they got caught and they could lose their livelihood. It isn't worth it.

Tommy also said that a cleaning crew comes out after every visit to spruce up the cabins and reset them for the next set of guests. Those crews are counted—because the new owners are reportedly very serious about not allowing any strays on the island to bother their guests—and it would've been impossible for someone to be on Halo Island without someone else knowing about it.

But what other explanation is there?

Right when I could tell that the crew would rather stay in denial than protect ourselves, I made sure to mention that I swore I saw a shadowy figure walking along the shore last night.

It's a fib. A tiny one. If I actually said the figure was leaving Summer and Tyler's cabin—that odds are I saw the *killer*—I could only imagine Tommy's overprotective reaction. He'd probably toss me on his back, dive into the Pacific, and swim the fifteen miles back to shore while racing sharks if he knew that.

So I don't tell him. What would it help? We already know we have a killer. At least, this way, the others know that the killer was close enough that he could get to Tyler.

He could get to *any* of us.

Tommy did give me a strange look when I did, but instead of acting like I'd probably imagined that, he used that as further proof that we weren't alone. And though he doesn't go so far as to suggest we try to outswim a great white shark, he does have a different plan.

He was going to find the killer and neutralize the psycho himself. I tried to get him to change his mind, but when Chase offered to go with him… when Chase ducked into his cabin and came back with a six-chambered *revolver*… the most I could do was agree to lock myself into the cabin while Chase and Tommy went looking for a monster.

Do I want to know why Chase has a gun? Not really. Right now, with someone hunting us, I'm just glad he does. Same for Tommy's switchblade. We need to be able to protect ourselves.

Then again, maybe that's what Chase has been doing. After getting jumped as a teen, beaten so badly that both of his legs were broken, carrying the gun on him was his way to get over it.

To move on.

Why is it so hard to move on?

That's what I'm thinking at this very second. Alone in the cabin that's quickly beginning to feel like a cage, I'm pacing the front room, waiting for Tommy to come back.

Night fell about an hour ago. It's dark. As beautiful as the weather is, the island itself is foreboding. It hungers for blood and it's already been fed at least once. Maybe twice if my suspicions about Vee's fall being more than an accident are valid.

I'm alone. If Tommy had it his way, I wouldn't be. The guys tried to convince us girls to hunker down in one of the cabins together. Safety in numbers, I guess. But when Summer conveniently had another mute attack, shaking her head while leaving Madison to explain that they'd prefer to stay together without me, I didn't argue.

Tommy locked me in. He kissed me goodbye, promised he'd be back as soon as they killed the creep killing *us*, then made me swear not to open the door to anyone. The cabins might be rustic-looking on the outside, but these aren't the type of doors you can kick in. You need a key, which is why Tommy took ours with him, but just in case, I move the couch up against the door.

I can't watch another movie. When it seems like I'm

living in a horror film all of a sudden, most of the cabin's collection is a huge turn-off.

Besides, I've spent the last couple of hours obsessively checking the window. I don't think I'll be able to breathe again until I see Tommy and Chase returning in one piece. They have to. There are two of them, each with a weapon, and I don't know what the killer wants with us or what they're doing out there, but I have faith in… well, Tommy, at least.

And a gun.

I have faith in the gun.

So why aren't they back yet?

For the hundredth time, I move next to the window, peering out into the darkness. Only one other cabin has a light on: Madison's. I see a light in the window, plus the one over the porch that wasn't on before. They must've flipped it so that they could see more easily outside, too.

That's not all the light does.

The gauzy yellow reach of the porch light illuminates a shadowy figure standing right in front of *Madison*'s cabin. Something catches on the item they're holding in their right hand. It flashes, like a reflection, but from this distance, I can't see what it is.

I also can't see *who* it is.

Is it the same figure from last night? Something in the way they move makes me think so, but it's familiar in another way. Almost like I *know* who that is—

I press my forehead against the glass, cupping my eyes to see better. I'm not too worried about the figure noticing me watching them. We have windows made of supposedly bulletproof glass, plus two impenetrable locked doors.

Who is that?

I can't tell. Their face… it's still shadowed.

Their steps start out slow. Easy. Leisurely. Like they have all the time in the fucking world, but they decided to stroll on down to *my* cabin. As soon as their pace picks up, I'm pretty sure they did catch me staring.

They can't get me. I tell myself that again as the figure eats up the distance between Madison's cabin and mine.

They can't, and because I'm so sure I'm safe in here, I don't move away from the window as the killer comes to a stop right in front of it.

They tilt their head.

I stop breathing as I get my first good look at the killer on Halo Island.

No wonder I couldn't pick out their features from the shadows.

They don't *have* any.

The killer is wearing a mask. A matte black plastic one, with holes for the eyes, slits for the nose, and nothing for the mouth. With the hood of his *black* hooded sweat-shirt—not blue, I think, not *blue*, but does it matter—up over his hair, I can't see if he has curls. The shadows make it difficult to tell if his eyes are brown or blue or green. I don't even know if it *is* a man that's out there, just on the other side of the window. The only spot of him not covered in black fabric or a mask is his hands. At the very least, I can tell our killer is white.

But I also know one other very important thing.

He's holding a knife in his right hand. I can't miss that. And when he slowly lifts up his left, I can't miss what he's holding in that one, either.

It's a *cabin key*.

WELCOME TO
HALO ISLAND
'til death
do we part...

TWELVE
RUN

How did he get it?

I give myself two seconds—*one, two*—to wonder how the masked figure outside my window got the key that only Tommy had before realization slams into me. He has the key. That means the killer can get into the cabin.

They can get *me*.

Fuck, no.

I only agreed to stay put because Tommy assured me it would be safe. I could grab a makeshift weapon from somewhere in here, but does that mean I'm as strong as this masked killer? He has a knife.

I wish I had Chase's gun.

I don't. I don't have Tommy's switchblade, either, but you know what I do have? Two good feet and a pair of running shoes that I am so fucking grateful that I didn't take off earlier.

I guess, deep down, I expected that the guys would find something, and I'd have to dash outside at a moment's notice. I definitely didn't expect that I'd become the masked killer's next victim—and I'm not planning on it, either.

The couch should buy me some time. Even if the killer opens the door with the key, he has to climb over it or move it or something. Unless he goes to the back, but since that's where I'm dashing to, I really hope not.

In horror movies, the heroine's hands always seem to stop working right when she's fleeing for her life. Doors she's opened a million times before getting stuck, or if she's carrying her phone or her keys, she's going to inevitably drop them.

Not this chick. I didn't grab my phone, I don't have any keys, and thank fucking God, the door unlocks easily. I turn the knob, fling it out, and jump down the three steps that lead up to the back porch before I'm *flying*.

I feel a teensy bit bad that I'm leaving Madison and Summer to the mercy of the killer, but as long as they were smart enough to keep their doors locked and not go off into the creepy dark woods, they should be fine. I asked Tommy if all the keys were the same; after all, that would defeat their purpose. They're not. Each key is for a different cabin, so either I was his next target—or the killer had someone else's key and used it to spook me into fleeing.

It's possible. I sure as hell didn't stick around to see if

the cabin key worked. Right now, I have to save my own ass. Two people are dead—

My hands fly to my face as I burst into a copse of trees and find another broken body on the ground.

Three people are dead…

This one is worse.

The scene is perfectly staged. I'd been running through the dark woods blind for a few minutes. Stray branches and half-dead bushes tore at my hair, at my skin, but I didn't give a shut. Adrenaline spurred me forward, and with the full moon overhead granting me enough light to make out *something*, I trampled through the trees, dead grass and a few fallen leaves crunching under my feet, without slamming face-first into a tree trunk.

But now… either my eyes have grown accustomed to the gloom, or the clearing is perfectly positioned to allow the moonlight to illuminate the patch of grass and dirt beneath it… because I see her with enough time to stop short before I run right over her.

I know from the faint blonde stripes in her hair that I'm looking at Summer Kaye. She's on her belly, and from the small distance between us, I could almost pretend she had passed out after a night at one of Gull-haven's local watering holes. Summer could never hold her liquor, but except for the first night, I don't think she's had another sip.

She's also immovably still.

In the back of my mind, I hear Chase saying that I

shouldn't touch the body. That's for the cops, and any tampering of the crime scene could make us all look suspicious. Screw that. I'm being chased by a maniac in a mask. I need to know what I'm up against.

I should've listened to that little voice.

Summer is dead. Like, I *knew* that, but when I grab her hand, she's already cool to the touch. When did I last see her? A couple of hours, at least, and she could've been dead nearly as long.

She's heavy, too. I have to use both hands to grab her and flip her over, and when I do?

I regret it.

There's a gaping hole in her throat. Anything from the chest down seems untouched, except for the stray blood drops that cover her blouse. It's clear that that's what killed her, but while she's clean from chest down, her eyes are wide and gaping, and her chin…

Her chin is *coated* in blood.

What the…

That's not all. Her lips seem sunken in, and when I make another mistake and lower my head to get a better look, I can tell that the source of the blood on her chin is coming from her mouth.

You know what they say about curiosity killing the cat? In this case, it has Cyn's stomach churning because, when I gingerly open her mouth to understand why there's so much blood, I gag and fall backward when I get it.

Her tongue is *missing*.

The masked killer must've pulled her by her highlighted hair, bared her throat, *slit* it, and for a little coup de grace, that insane fucker *cut out her tongue*.

I've got to go. Summer Kaye was a bitch, but with all that blood… he did it while she was *alive*.

If he did that to her, what is he going to do to me?

As if my fear managed to summon him, right as I pull myself back up, he's here. He's *here*. He steps out of the trees, stalking toward me, and I'm so fucking scared, I nearly piss myself.

Then he says one word, and I think I might have.

"*Cyn.*"

Oh my God. Oh my *God*.

He knows my name.

How does he know my name?

Did he stalk us? Learn everything about us? Discover our dark secrets and decide we needed to die one by one on Halo Island?

Holy shit. I thought I was in a horror movie. Have I found myself in Agatha Christie's infamous murder mystery instead?

It doesn't matter. I outpaced him this far, and the only reason the killer caught up to me was because I couldn't bring myself to leave Summer behind.

But I have to. Besides, I can't help her now. She's gone, and before the killer can make a break for me, so am I.

DO I GO BACK TO THE CABIN?

I want to. The killer is in the woods, and there's a chance I can beat him back to the shore. I don't know if any of the other cabins are locked—or if Madison stayed behind while Summer went looking for the guys—but he had one key. What are the odds he has more than one? Six cabins… I could take my chance.

And just as I'm debating whether I should turn back, I hear a crack behind me and pour on as much speed as I'm capable of.

I keep seeing him behind me. I thought I was outpacing him, but I have to admit the reality is he's fucking toying with me. He lets me see him when he wants to, and after how easily I stumbled on Summer's body, I'm thinking that had to be on purpose.

I'm one hundred percent sure I'm right when, about ten minutes later—that seem like ten excruciating *hours*— I find another body.

The *fourth* one.

This one is testing my stomach. I thought it was made of iron. I've seen some gnarly shit in my time, and after both Tyler and Summer's murders, I thought I was numb to *anything*.

And then I see what happened to Madison Powell.

She's not in the cabin. Whatever brought the two of them out into the woods to be slaughtered, they came together—and died separately in two very brutal ways.

Madison's naked. The twisted part of my brain that responds to dark humor—like how, if anyone asks how my mom is, I'd tell them she's down under… six feet under —thinks: Huh. She probably would've enjoyed knowing that she got to go naked.

Her legs are spread, but they're the only part of her not touched. I'd like to think the psycho masked killer didn't stop to rape her before he strung her up, but who the hell knows? She's naked, her body an 'X', with both arms and legs tied between two trees about six feet off the ground.

And her body…

Ribbons. That's the only word I can think of right now. She's been stabbed so viciously, cut up so expertly, that hunks of flesh are spilling over like fucking *ribbons*. Maybe she was wearing clothes before the killer got to her. They probably got sliced to bits as someone *peeled* her apart.

Don't puke, Cyn. Puking will just slow you down. Get away, I tell myself. He knows Madison is here. He *put* her here. He found you by Summer's body—

Because he wanted me to see his handiwork? Because he wanted me to know what I should expect to happen to me next?

I don't know. I don't *know*. But he was there when I stopped to gape in horror at Summer, and while this is even worse, I have to go.

I can't stay—

He steps out from the shadows. His knife is high, and I strangle my scream.

"Don't run from me—"

Too late, psycho. I'm already gone.

Summer's dead. Madison's dead.

And if I can't escape the masked slasher chasing me, I have no doubt in my mind that I'm next.

I run. With every step, with every turn, I sense him at my back. Because of his dark clothes, because of his black mask, I can't see him until he's too close. He seems to be everywhere, or maybe I'm running in circles. I'm careful to avoid the spots where I found Summer and Madison's bodies, but what if I stumble on Chase next?

What about Tommy?

I can't go back to the cabins. I have to outrun the killer, but when my adrenaline isn't enough to support my flagging legs, I know that that's unlikely.

I was never an athlete like Clay and Tommy. I haven't willingly gone for a run since high school ended, and that was more than ten years ago. It's a miracle I made it this far, but despite my best intentions of being like Sydney Prescott, I really am Casey Becker instead.

And just as I have that thought, he appears. Like Ghostface, but not, he stalks me from behind so I don't even see him coming before I'm snared.

He grabs my arms, lifting me off the ground. I find a renewed burst of adrenaline, but it's worthless. His grip —and it has to be a man from the voice I heard before— is so strong, I wouldn't be surprised if I have bruises in the morning… and then I realize: I've been caught by a masked killer. There won't be a tomorrow morning for me.

At least I died around the same time as Clay, I think; depending on if it's past midnight at this point or not, it might even be the same day.

October 28th.

Of course it's October 28th.

I'm resigned to my inevitable death. There's no use in trying to fight, especially in his grip. He's holding onto me like he's afraid I'll start running again. I would, too. I totally would. But his hold is a vice, even as he manhandles me, maneuvering me around so that I'm forced to look up at that terrifyingly blank mask.

I would've preferred a hockey mask, I think with just a touch of hysteria. A painted version of William Shatner's head, like Michael Myers had in *Halloween*. A skeleton mask. The one from *The Purge*. Any of those would be better because then I could pretend that I'm in a horror movie, and that there might still be someone coming to save me.

But I've never seen such a featureless mask before. It hides everything, giving nothing away, and the flat, matte color of the black mask makes me feel like I'm looking at death.

This isn't a movie. This is real life. I'm going to die on Halo Island, and as I close my eyes, waiting for the knife to plunge into my chest, I can't help but admit that that's kind of fitting.

To die on Halo Island—

The killer shakes. It takes a second for me to realize that he's… he's *laughing*.

I open my eyes a crack and see that the mask?

It's *gone*.

And that's not all.

I know that face.

I know that fucking *face*.

As handsome and as smug as ever, he grins at me.

I know that grin, too.

"Silly Cyn. You should've known better than to run from your husband."

Husband?

Husband?

Clay.

THE IMAGE I HAVE IN MY HEAD OF CLAYTON RIVERS IS A fresh-faced twenty-two-year-old boy with thick sandy brown hair and pretty green eyes. He was the boy next door. Handsome. Hard-working. *Mine*.

He was the man who worshiped the ground I walked on, who loved me, who denied me nothing, and who simply disappeared one terrible October morning.

Dead, I tell myself. I thought he was dead.

But though Clay looks older… harder… damn it, *sexier*… he's not dead.

He's also not my husband anymore.

Once he's sure that I recognize him—once he can sense that I'm not about to run… yet—he sets me down. I take a few hurried steps away from him, and then I *stare*.

His eyes are darker than I remember. He's not as scruffy as Tommy, though my Clay was always clean-shaven. This man looks like he hasn't seen a razor in a week. His hair is longer. Shaggier. There are hard lines that weren't there before.

He never had any freckles, either, but beneath the moonlight, I see a few stray dots.

My stomach lurches.

Blood.

That's *blood*.

He has a knife. Between the black outfit and the weapon, I know he has to be the one responsible for killing Tyler.

And Madison.

And Summer…

Only… Clay's *dead*. Or he's supposed to be. I thought it was Tommy if anyone, or maybe a stranger, but I know that face… that body… this *man* intimately.

It's Clayton Rivers, and I have no idea how this is possible.

Do I run? Faint? Throw myself at him, sobbing? Scream?

No. I stand there and stare as he waits for me to do *something*.

When I can finally speak again, I say the most obvious thing I can: "You're *dead*."

"'Reports of my death have been greatly exaggerated'," he quotes, a hint of a smile softening his features as he lifts his knife, pressing the tip of the blade against his bottom lip. "Surprise, Cyn. Did you miss me?"

I don't answer that. I can't. If I admit that I missed this man every single fucking day after he disappeared *and he was alive the whole damn time*… no. *No.* He doesn't get to ask me questions. He left me. Now he wants to reappear and fucking *terrorize* me?

I don't know who this man is, but he's not *my* husband.

"Who are you?" I demand. "What are you doing here? There isn't supposed to be anyone else on the island. How did you get here?"

The Clay I knew loved it when I was inquisitive. He was even more pleased when I made demands, showing him my dominant side—so long as he could still take control in bed, of course.

So when he smiles and my heart nearly fucking breaks again to see that it's tainted, it's cruel, but it's still Clay's smile… I don't want to believe that I know this man. That it's *him*. I don't want to… but how can I, especially when he knows my name—and that's not all?

"Easy, babe." *Babe…* why does he think he can call me 'babe'? Here, on Halo Island, where he… "I took the first ferry over at ten in the morning on Friday. I gave the old man Aaron's name." He chuckles, and it's so dark, shivers run down my spine. "Fuck knows he wasn't going to need the ride."

What? We didn't get the message from Aaron that he wasn't joining us until *two*. "How did you know he wasn't coming?"

Another chuckle, even darker. "I made sure he wasn't. Then I handed his phone to some drunk waiting for the bar down the street from the harbor to open. Gave him a hundred bucks to send the pre-typed message and dump the phone. Told him there would be five hundred more if he did it and that me and my buddies were playing a game so I'd know." His eyes light up. "Looks like I owe him the five hundred, huh?"

I made sure he wasn't…

"Wait. You… you killed Aaron? He's dead, too?"

What?

WELCOME TO
HALO ISLAND
'til death
do we part...

THIRTEEN

CRAWL

A second later, I can't help but think: duh. Like, really? I only just saw firsthand what he did to two of our other friends. Why am I so shocked that Aaron might've been another one of them?

But I am. Probably because, now that I know who was under that mask, I can't imagine Clay doing any of that.

Look at him. He's more than happy to explain —

"He was the first. The easiest. When you want to drown someone, just do it. Hold them under—"

I can't hear this. Not with the memory of Vee's broken body, Tyler's mutilated chest, Summer's bloody face, and Madison strung up like a doll all running through my head....

"*Stop.*"

Surprisingly, he does, even as his voice takes on a

teasing lilt. "You sure you don't want to hear more, baby? Fuck, I missed talking to you. That's not all I missed, either, but… you look good, Cyn. Better up close." He twirls his knife. "Maybe even better on the inside."

I jut my chin up at him, hiding the fact my knees are knocking. "You going to kill me, Clay?"

"Maybe," is his short answer. "But let's go in order first. How 'bout that? I said Aaron was the first. Now that I think of it, though, he might not have been the easiest. That was probably Violet."

Vee.

"What about Vee?"

He mimes a push. "Whoops. Violet lost her step. Too bad. So sad." My fucking God, he's lost it. That's what happened while he was gone. Clay… he went absolutely insane, and every word that follows just makes me more and more sure I'm right. "I had something better planned for her, but she was always too nosy for her own good. She had to go snooping. I couldn't resist." He shakes his head. "She snapped something on the way down and never came back up."

I can't believe I'm hearing this.

"She was your friend," I gasp.

"My *friend* never would've told Chase Whitmore that you were into him. That you talked about wanting to fuck him. My *friend* wouldn't have passed him enough shots to work up liquid courage to make his move and tug your head down into his lap after he yanked his cock out. My *friend* wouldn't have spread rumors all over town that the girl I'd do anything for would go under the bleachers and suck dick for ten bucks. I followed you everywhere, Cyn. Even back then. It was Tommy for you until you were mine. That bitch ruined your reputation with lies. She was never our friend."

"She… she did that?"

Clay nods, letting it sink in.

My world feels like it's spinning off its axis. I thought it did when Clay removed his mask, but hearing that *Vee* set me up? "I… but *why*?"

"Because Summer Kaye asked her to. Because Summer Kaye thought that would be enough for Tommy to choose her over you. Because Summer Kaye doesn't know when to keep her goddamn mouth shut." He smirks. "She couldn't try to say shit to me when I was cutting her tongue out, I'll tell you that much."

Summer… "You killed her, too?"

"Of course. And don't worry, baby. She offered to suck my cock if I spared her. With the mask on, she had no clue who I was, but she was ready to drop to her knees for me anyway to save her ass. That was enough of a reason for the tongue to go. It's only ever been you for me. Even while we were apart, there was no one else. And she thought I'd risk pissing you off by letting *her* touch me? Never. If I'm taking pussy as a bribe, there's only one I want."

Why does a small frisson of pleasure wind its way

through me when I hear that, wherever he was while he was gone, he stayed loyal?

Why does an echoing sensation of guilt follow on its heels when I think about how I went back to Tommy?

I shake my head, knocking those thoughts out of it.

"How… how do you know all that? About Summer? And Vee?"

"Easy. Chase told me."

Chase told him? Wait… "Did he know—"

"That I was alive?" Clay provides.

Again with the obvious: "Well, you're not dead."

He's not *dead*.

"Of course not." He bangs his plastic mask against his thigh. "There's a reason I keep this on, babe—"

"I'm not your babe," I snap. "Not anymore. You died." I saw the crime scene photos. I begged and sobbed until Detective O'Halloran felt sorry for me and let me see them. The blood… "You *died*, Clay."

"Then call me fucking Lazarus because I'm back." He moves closer to me, reaching out, fisting the air when I stumble away from him. "I'm back for you, Cyn. For revenge. And nothing is going to keep me from you again."

No. What? *No.*

Revenge? For what? For Chase trying to force me to suck his dick when I was seventeen? For Vee… fucking Vee… planting the idea in his drunken head that I might actually cheat on Tommy with *him*? For Summer using SA to break Tommy and me up?

If all that is true, then why the fuck does *Clay* care? He left me. I can't even bring myself to ask why because then I'll have to face what I think I always knew: death could steal my husband from me, but if he didn't die, then that meant I wasn't important enough.

That I was *never* important—

"And you've been holding onto all that info for how long?" Did he just find out? Is that why he came back? He moved on, lived his life, but a tiny bit of leftover affection turned him into *this*?

Into a masked killer on a secluded island, days before Halloween?

"Does it matter?"

He has no idea how much *everything* matters to me.

The old Clay would have. But this new one?

"For how fucking long?" I ask again.

His expression is one of daring. Of defiance. "For as long as it took to make sure I could get the perfect revenge for you."

"So you killed all my old high school friends? What next?" I demand. "Me?"

His lips curve. "How's Tommy, Cyn?"

All of my defiance dies a death even quicker than the others when he asks me that.

He moves a few steps closer. "I knew you'd end up with him, ya know. You've always loved him. Didn't you, baby?"

I loved *Clay*.

"You left me." My words are softer than I intended them to be, full of pain even if I'd rather conceal it.

He hardens his jaw. "I had to."

No. He didn't.

He steps closer. I stumble back again. "Clay… what happened to you?"

"It's very simple. I wanted my wife. I couldn't have her. Not yet. I had to fucking *wait*. But I know you, Cyn. You'd throw it in my face that I had to leave at all."

"You didn't *have* to—"

"I did. You'll understand soon enough why. All I've ever done is protect you, even if it had to be from myself."

Well, I'm thinking he didn't do that great of a job considering I'm face-to-face with a formerly masked killer who chased me through the woods.

I gulp. "What else did you protect me from?" I think of the two bodies that I'm pretty sure he guided me past on purpose. "The mean girls? Is that it?"

"From the rumors," Clay says flatly. "*All* of them."

I take a deep breath. "Because I'm the one who found my mom all those years ago."

And Chase. We can't forget about what happened with Chase…

He jerks his head at me. Yes.

Summer fucking Kaye. She told everyone I did it, that I killed my mom, that I led Chase on and tried to start shit between three close friends. No one believed her, not really, but there were enough curious stares that I was more than happy to leave Gullhaven with Clay when he asked me. Even if I didn't think it wasn't possible for me to survive without him myself, I would've gone.

But look at that. I *did* survive. I made it five terrible fucking years without him, and *now* he's back?

He faked his death. That much is obvious. Suddenly, I don't care *why*, either, though I do say, "What else is new? Since I came back to Gullhaven with Tommy, they all thought I killed you, too." I make a sound in the back of my throat that could be interpreted as me joking, but I mean it when I add, "I thought about it. For making me live without you, if you hadn't been dead, I would've. Instead, I thought about going after who hurt you. But I couldn't find any leads. Of course not. It's so obvious now. *You* did it. So maybe I *should* kill you."

"You wouldn't."

"Why not?"

He grins. God, I'm a sucker for that grin… "I'm your husband."

I'll do anything to wipe that smug grin off of his face. "'Til death do we part, remember? You died."

He doesn't have an answer for that, though I did what I accomplished.

His smile is gone.

And, for the second time, I ask, "What now? Are you going to kill me, Clayton?"

He lifts his knife. I try not to, but I flinch.

"What? You'd kill me. Isn't that what you just said, baby? Maybe you're not that appreciative of my gifts. My *sacrifices*. Of my offerings…" He hardens his expression to the point he's unrecognizable. "Deny me, Cyn. See what happens."

I close in on myself.

He looms, taking one step, then another until we're less than a foot apart. I have to tilt my head back to meet the fury in his gaze.

"You promised me your loyalty," he grates out between clenched teeth. A muscle tics in his cheek. "How long was I in the ground before you let Tommy fuck you the first time?"

My head jerks as if he slapped me. It's my fault? He disappeared. After three years, I found solace with an old boyfriend—and it's *my* fault?

"I thought you were dead," I snap at him. "You were *supposed* to be dead."

He takes the back of my head in his hands, cradling it, pulling me closer while ducking his, forcing our foreheads to touch. "Oh, Cyn," he murmurs. "Did our vows mean so little to you? In sickness and in health… I lost my mind, and I lost my wife. You should've waited for me. I *wanted* you to."

"You should've told me," I whisper.

"I should've," he agrees, releasing me.

Once he does, I move until a good five feet are keeping us apart now. I'm so confused. Worse, part of me is ecstatic that Clay's here. All I ever wanted was my husband back—but this is not the man I remember.

So he knows. I suspected as much. In order to

arrange this… to get on the ferry, to even know we were coming to Halo Island in the first place… to go through with this insane plan of revenge of his, he had to have known about Tommy.

I bite down on my bottom lip, wipe my damp hands on my jeans, then blurt out the only thought currently on my mind: "If you hate me so much for getting with Tommy while you were gone, is he next? Or am I?"

He sucks in a breath. His cheeks hollow, and I see something flicker in his eyes that I know all too well. "I don't hate you. So get that out of your head. As for Tommy…" He lifts his knife again, tilting it, using it to reflect the moonlight so I can't miss it. "I haven't made up my mind yet. What will you do for me if I decide to spare him? Another chase, maybe? See what happens when I catch you again?"

Is that what this is all about? Is that why he picked now? Picked this place?

Picked *me?*

He wants a timid heroine? To play out his masked slasher fantasies this Halloween?

Fine.

I'll do anything to get that knife from him before he kills again.

I'll do anything to keep him from going after Tommy.

Clay's here for me. I'm his wife, after all. I can't save Vee. Tyler. Summer. Madison… but I can fucking save Tommy.

I make a big display of folding my hands in front of

my chest, plumping up my cleavage. Then, in a breathless voice, I tell him, "Anything you want, baby."

He closes his eyes, big body shuddering at my easy acquiescence.

Clay doesn't move other than that. I *could* run, but he'll catch me. He still has the knife. I'm not strong enough to overpower him, but if he gives me the chance… there are other ways for me to bring this man to his knees.

Keeping the same ingenue tone, I ask, "What were you doing anyway? All that time you were gone… what were you doing?"

His eyes snap open. "Counting down the minutes until I could be with my wife again."

The heat in his gaze has me second guessing myself.

I don't understand any of this. I simply don't *understand*. He *died*. But he didn't die. He faked his death somehow, for reasons that I don't know, and the man I lost five years ago is now a *masked murderer*?

But he's still Clay, and I see a hint of my old husband when he dabs his bottom lip with his tongue before putting his knife away. I notice the sheath on his hip before my attention is stolen as he unbuttons his jeans, yanks down his fly, and reveals the hard cock he kept tucked behind his pants.

He braces his boots in the dirt. "On your knees, Cyn."

I start to walk toward him, but he shakes his head. "No. I said, on your knees."

I drop down to one, then the other.

"Good girl. You know better than to refuse, don't you? That'll make this so much more fun for the both of us."

Somehow, I don't think so—and I'm right when, in the next breath, he orders: "Crawl."

WELCOME TO
HALO ISLAND
'til death
do we part...

FOURTEEN
MERCY

I freeze, meeting the renewed dare in his gaze.

He nods. "Crawl, Cyn. If you want my forgiveness... if you want your husband's cock... you'll crawl for it."

Part of me wants to spit at him and refuse. I don't think he'll really kill me after all, but can I say the same thing about Tommy? For all I know, my boyfriend's already dead, but if there's a chance he isn't...

I crawl. My back arched, ass sticking out, I still hold my head high as I crawl on my hands and knees through the woods of Halo Island to reach Clay's thick, hard cock.

He's fisting it, eyes fixated on every move I make. As I rise up on my knees, staring up through my lashes at him, I see his chest is heaving.

He wants this so bad.

I can use that.

"You're the only pussy I've ever had," he says roughly. "But you can't say the same about my cock, can you?"

Uh-oh.

Maybe I can't.

He's unpredictable. Ruthless. A killer.

I rest on my heels. "Clay—"

"Shh, Cyn. Not right now. If you're going to open your mouth, I don't want to hear excuses. I just want you to suck me off. Here." He grabs his cock, angling it so that I can bob my head down and take him between my lips. He waits until I do, then throws back his head and groans. "See? A mouth like this? It can make me forgive a lot.

"But can it make me forget you cheated?" He strokes my temple before lowering his hand, closing my jaw around him. "Suck me like you mean it and we'll see."

I've blown Clay thousands of times. I know what he likes and how he likes it. It's almost habit, and as though five years haven't passed at all, I do just that.

I can't be doing that great of a job, though, because even as I cup his sac and hollow my cheeks, using every trick I have to make my husband lose his mind, all he does is degrade me for moving on.

Does he remember how much it turns me on for him to do that? Or is this how he really feels? I'm not sure, but with that knife as close as it is, just on the waistband of his jeans, I don't rise to the bait. I let him say whatever he wants while I continue to bob my head on his cock.

"How long was I gone before you were fucking my best friend? How long before you took his cock like a dirty little whore? Did he make you scream, Cyn? The same way I did?" He fingers the hilt of his knife before twining his fingers through my hair. "I can make you scream now."

Fucking hell. I'm not even getting any stimulation out of this and my panties are *soaked*. When we were married, we didn't get the chance to explore alternative lifestyles like BDSM—there wasn't enough time for us— but I never came harder than when Clay took me like I was his property. His blonde sex doll who existed to be fucked by him.

Like he owned me, like he would die if he couldn't shoot his load inside of me.

I get that sensation at this very moment, and even though I tell myself I agreed to this for Tommy's sake, I forget all about him—until Clay speaks up again.

"Did you let Tommy fuck your mouth like this?" he asks, pumping in and out of me as I relax my jaw, letting him do just *that* now. "Did you worship his cock like it's your god and the fucking floor is your altar?"

Mouth stuffed full of Clay, I can't answer him, and I also know better than to let his dick slip from my mouth while he's using me.

I can tell myself it's to save Tommy's life all I want, but I'd be lying if I said I didn't miss this. Didn't miss *Clay*.

"My pretty little whore." He runs his fingers through

my hair again. "I know how much you like to fuck. Tell me… while I was gone, did you give him all of your holes?"

I moan around his cock. I don't mean to, but when I remember exactly what Clay means when he says 'all' of my holes…

"Well? Tell me, baby."

I shake my head.

His eyes are insane, but they're also bright at that realization. "Ah. So there are still some things you know belong to your husband."

He's happy to hear that, but he's also on the edge of coming. I can sense it in the way he's just about touching the back of my throat, enjoying the sensation as I gag on his length, but he keeps fucking me while I cling to his thighs.

I expect him to keep going until he shoots his load into my throat. Only, that's the old Clay. The new Clay?

He taps my shoulder, the universal sign to release a cock during a blowjob.

Confused, but not willing to push him right now, I let him slip out from between my lips.

His voice is husky and full of need as he commands:

"Take off your sweater."

Puzzled but still willing to do what I'm told at this moment, I shrug off the red sweater.

He smiles when he sees my bra, but then his gaze dips, and his expression turns predatory. "You're still wearing my ring, Cyn."

Fuck. How did I forget? If I wanted to pretend I couldn't care less about Clay, taking his ring off might've been a good start… and then I nearly choke when I notice that Clay… he still has a wedding band on the fourth finger of his left hand.

Husband…

If he notices that I saw his ring, he doesn't react to it. "Maybe there's hope for you yet. And because you sucked my dick like a good girl, you get a present. I'm going to give you a pretty necklace to go along with it."

He punctuates his statement by grabbing his cock, twisting it, stroking it, tugging until, before I know it, he's coming. Jets of semen shoot out of him, and he makes sure to get it all over my neck and chest.

When he's done, he crouches down, using the flat of his hand to rub in my brand new pearl necklace.

"You belong to me," he tells me in a tone that says he won't be dissuaded from this. "You always have. You always will."

That's what he thinks.

Coming down from his orgasm, Clay forgot for a moment who he was dealing with. Sure, I'll crawl to get what I want… but I'm no demure heroine.

I can fake it, though. Simpering, pulling an expression that tells him I'm dying for his forgiveness—and maybe his cock again—I whimper. "I was lonely. You were dead."

He strokes the edge of my jaw. "Does that give you permission to cheat? To fuck another man?"

"I didn't cheat. You left me, Clay. You were gone!"

"I know, baby. But I'm back. Fuck. My insecurities are my own problems. I'll get over them. I'll make 'em up to you."

He can try. "You can't blame me for trying to move on," I tell him.

He leans closer to me, giving me the perfect angle I need. "You weren't supposed to. You're not *allowed*."

And that does it.

Shooting my hand out, I grab Clay's knife by the hilt. I rear back, slashing wildly, kicking out at him when I make contact with his side. He grunts painfully, and I'm sure I got him, but I swipe again just in case to knock him back.

"You don't always get to tell me what to do," I tell him as he lands on his ass, clutching his side.

I drop the knife, grab my sweater, and *run*.

He laughs. Though I'm sure he'll be coming right after me, it's his voice that chases me through the woods first.

"There's the Cyn I went through hell to get back to," he calls out. "Keep running. Just know you're only making me want you more, baby."

I ALWAYS THOUGHT GUNSHOTS RANG OUT LIKE fireworks: short bursts of loud noise that leave an echo in their wake.

In a way, they are. But movies don't really sell how *loud* they are. When the two gunshots went off in quick succession, the noise scared me so badly that I missed a step, fell on my knees, and had to push back up again to keep running.

I expected Clay to run me down. Sure, he was joking, laughing, *teasing* after I slashed at him—further proof that he's lost his mind—but after everything he said… he's coming for me. My only hope is to outlast him. Make it until morning. Get on the ferry and survive.

I'll be the final girl. Halo Island won't be the death of me.

That's what I'm thinking a split second before the shots exploded.

Bang.

Bang.

I'm thinking about how I *am* the final girl since Vee, Summer, and Madison are all murdered when the shots ring out, I go down, and all I can think now is that, in the horror movie, don't stumble. Don't fall. Don't look back.

Don't run off in the direction of gunshots.

But I have to. Tommy's out here in the woods somewhere. At least, I have to believe that because if Clay got to him before I could warn him… No. He's out here. He's safe.

Or he was.

Gunshots. I heard gunshots.

Chase had a gun. Unless he and Tommy got separated, they should be together.

I cling to that as I run. It's nowhere near where I left Clay, and right when I'm beginning to think my ears are off and I went in the totally wrong direction, I hear a strangled noise like an animal dying.

I immediately stop running. My heavy breathing makes it hard to hear, so I swallow it, forcing it down, going light-headed as I choose listening to my surroundings over trying to catch my breath.

There it is again. Right ahead of me—

Oh. My. God.

I thought it was bad when I walked into Tyler's room and the rancid odor slapped me in the face. As I push past the trees, it's a hundred times worse—and we're outside. Why does it smell so bad?

I get my answer when I see another body.

Fuck.

The white polo tells me it's Chase unless, for some reason, he and Tommy changed. I look for his head, but it's hard to tell from where I am. He's curled up in the fetal position, head tucked, so if he has curls, I don't know.

I have to know.

What made that noise, I wonder. Did an animal come upon this scene, thinking it was getting a free meal from one of my friends, then catch the scent of death and absolute putrid shit on the air?

I'm breathing through my mouth until I get used to it. Can I get used to it? It doesn't matter. I just need to see who this is—

A death rattle. A groan. A wordless plea.

"Holy shit!"

That noise came from the body!

I run. Common sense says I should run back the way I came, not toward the body, but if there's any chance it's Tommy…

It's not. It's Chase.

His face is white, drawn into a mask of agony. Blood bubbles at the corner of his mouth. From the front, I notice what I missed in the back: two bullet holes in his white polo shirt, each one on a different shoulder. He got shot with his own gun, considering that's the only weapon I see by his expensive loafer shoe.

But that's not the worst part.

He's curled up in the fetal position, not because of the gunshots that got him, but because he's cradling his…

His…

I heave. The smell's bad, but it's even worse when I look down and see parts of Chase Whitmore on the outside that should *always* be on the inside.

And he's still fucking alive? How?

I recoil. "Chase, oh my God… Chase? What happened to you?"

"Disembowelment," comes an answering voice. "Evisceration. Whatever you want to call it, someone cut him open like a fish, but it's not enough to die. Not right away, that is."

Torture. This is torture.

Aaron was drowned. Vee, pushed. Tyler probably died with the first stab to his heart. Summer had her throat cut—and her tongue cut out. Madison was slashed to ribbons. All quicker deaths, some more efficient than others.

But Chase…

"You did this to Chase? How?" The gunshots rang out from a different direction than where I left Clay. I know he didn't catch up to me right away, but how did he get over here, gut Chase, shoot Chase, *torture* Chase… it's not possible, but I don't want to hear it when Clay shrugs and says, "I didn't."

I snap. Dropping to the grass, I grab the gun where the killer must've left it. Rising back up, I lift it, aiming dead at Clay. "Stop fucking lying to me!"

He steps closer, making himself a better target. "You wouldn't dare."

My arms waver. The gun feels so heavy in my hands. So *wrong*. He's right, too. If I wanted to kill him, I could've. But when I see that smug face of his…

I'm shit with a gun. Why wouldn't I be? I'm a stay-at-home girlfriend who used to be a stay-at-home wife. I don't know how to use a gun—and that's a lie.

Does Clay know that I've gone to the range to kill some time? I don't know where he's been, but if he stalked me before setting this plan into motion, he might.

I keep the gun up.

He waits.

So I pull the trigger, careful to aim just over his head.

That way, I have plausible deniability when it doesn't hit him, and—

Shit.

Nothing happens.

I pull the trigger again, not even caring where I aim now. It clicks, but no bullet leaves the round.

It's *empty*.

"It had six chambers! That's what you said," I say accusingly to the whimpering lump at my feet. Then I feel awful, like the worst person in the whole goddamn world, and fold in on myself.

Meanwhile, Clay twists his knife, making the moonlight dance off the pristine metal.

Pristine? If he gutted Chase, wouldn't it be covered in blood? Did he have time to clean that up, too?

"See?" he says. "That's why I went with a knife. Sure, you can get the job done from farther away with the gun, but you run out of bullets or forget to reload when you're showing off to the girl of the week you're fucking, what then? The knife, on the other hand… it requires skill. Nerve. You gotta get close. You gotta not mind getting your hands dirty. Right, baby?"

"Shut up," I hiss. "You're sick. I can't… leave me alone, Clay. Leave me alone!"

"I can't. Don't you see that I can't? I thought I could. Since I knew I'd find my way back to you one day, I thought… a couple of years to make our marriage stronger? To make it so Cyn could *never* leave me? I thought I could do it." He gestures at his chest with his knife. "See this? This is what happens when I leave you alone."

Another terrible noise escapes Chase. His body jolted when I said Clay's name—almost as if, even in his agony, he's shocked to learn that my supposedly dead husband is here—and that noise is the death throes that wracked him as his body shook.

But then it dies, though Chase doesn't, not yet, and I swear I hear him whisper a name.

It's the last thing I want to do, but I throw Clay a quelling look, warning him not to say another fucking word, then crouch down by the thing that used to be Chase Whitmore.

His eyes are wide and staring, but he can still make out a name. "Tommy…"

"Shh," I say, trying to soothe him. "I'll find Tommy. It's going to be okay."

Clay snorts, the sick bastard enjoying this way too much. "Oh? So you're a liar, too, Cyn. Look. Let's make this clear. He's not okay. He's not going to be okay. It can take hours for him to die like this. Bullets to the shoulders. Guts on the grass. He's dead, and he knows it."

"*Tommy…*"

"He can still talk—"

"Of course. Because he's trying to tell you who did this to him." Ignoring my warning, Clay stomps closer, then kicks Chase in the knee. He whispered Tommy's name, but he howls in agony at the kick. Clay laughs. "Looks like Tommy finally got his revenge."

I goggle up at him as I push up to my feet. "What?"

Clay shrugs. "Fair enough. I did get the pleasure of breaking this prick's legs in high school. I wouldn't let Tommy help. He was too squeamish at the time, and I needed the outlet for my rage even then. Touching my girl, Chase? You had to know I couldn't let that stand." He scoffs. "You're just lucky I wasn't murdering then. That's a recent development." He glances at me. "For Tommy, too, it seems."

"But Chase isn't dead," I blurt out again.

"No," Clay agrees, offering me the hilt of his knife. "So why don't you finish the job?"

I step back. "Why would I do that?"

"Some might say it's mercy for an old friend. But we know better. It's for the same reason Tommy left him like this, then probably fired the gunshots for you to find him." He bares his teeth at me. "*Revenge.*"

I shake my head.

"Come on. You know you want to."

"I don't—"

"Yes. You do. Remember what it was like to have your face in his lap."

My stomach rebels, and not only because of what Tommy—not Tommy, *why* Tommy—did to Chase. "Clay, please—"

"He held you down, baby. Tried to fuck your mouth just like I did."

He's not listening to me, and that makes me angry. I

have the sudden urge to do the same. He's right. Chase is a goner, but Clay…

At the reminder of what we just did, I wipe my lips with the back of my hand. His semen is sticky on my chest, but until I can get away from Clay and wash it off, there's nothing I can do about that.

His eyes flash.

I glare back at him. "What?"

"Don't," Clay says, his voice a warning. "Don't wipe me off of you unless you want me to mark you all over again. Let him suffer if you want. Fuck it. Let him *watch* as I make you mine again."

I gasp. "You wouldn't."

"I would. Oh, baby. I *will*."

Chase whimpers again, but that's the only noise he makes.

But Clay's right about something. Chase *is* suffering. This is cruel. My Clay is fucking deranged, but he's never been *cruel*.

I stomp over to him.

He offers me the knife.

I take it, then shudder.

"If you want to make it quick, go for the throat. That's what I do."

Yeah. I know.

Fuck. Can I do this? I have nightmares about seeing my mother's body bobbing on the surface of the lake. The smell of Chase's guts will haunt me for the rest of my life. I don't need to add the sensation of drawing a blade across his throat, but the gun is empty because the dying idiot didn't reload his rounds before we came to Halo Island. Who knows. Maybe Tommy would've unloaded the entire chamber to get my attention and I would've been left in the same situation.

Of course, that's assuming this isn't all more fiction on Clay's part.

God, do I wish this was all fake…

"You won't do it?" I ask Clay, already knowing the answer.

He shakes his head. "Use the knife. Make it quick if you want, but unless you'd rather leave him like this…"

Got it.

Taking a shaky breath, I lower myself next to Chase again.

He has one more word for me: "*Please…*"

"You won't hurt anymore," I promise him.

"Or hurt anyone else, either," adds Clay in a sing-song voice.

WELCOME TO
HALO ISLAND
'til death
do we part...

FIFTEEN
MINE

That seals it for me. Maybe, later, I'll look back and think this whole night was a fucking nightmare, and that's all it was. A bad dream. How many times have I dreamed of Clay coming back like this? Well. No. Not like this, and that's exactly why it's a bad dream.

But Clay's right. Chase hurt me. He never said he was sorry. I don't realize how much that's fucked me up until right this very second. He never took ownership, and as a defense attorney, he's spent his fledgling career helping other people evade justice.

This time, I want a little myself.

I can pretend I'm doing this to show mercy. I can act squeamish, cover my eyes with my fingers, tell Clay that I can't… but the truth of the matter is, as I lower the knife to Chase's throat and slash, it's a lot easier to kill a man than it should be.

I don't even have a moment to reflect on it. With his guts all over the grass, my slice might've killed him, but it was really just the permission Chase Whitmore needed to let go. Whoever gutted him—and it has to be Clay, no matter what he said, because I can't believe it could be *Tommy*—is responsible for this death. I just freed him.

And that's enough to show me a side of Clay I've always known existed.

He's opened his jeans again. The zipper is down, the button wide open. While I finished poor Chase off, Clay reached his hand inside of his pants and pulled out his monstrous erection. Holy fuck. It seems even bigger than when he had me choking on it earlier.

He works it expertly, a plea in his voice as he calls out my name. "Cyn. I *need* you."

I meet his gaze. His murderous expression has melted away to one of lust. Of want. Of *desperation*.

And I'm pretty sure I know why.

Chase is dead. I killed him, and now Clay has his cock out, stroking himself, watching me with a look that says, if I don't give him what he wants, he might die himself for real this time.

I lick my lips, then hand the knife back to him. He takes it with his left hand, still stroking his length roughly with his right.

"I need you," he says again, more forceful this time. "I need all of you. I need you to be mine."

And I want this night to be over and for it all to have made some kind of sense. "What's in it for me?"

He laughs. "Oh, baby. I'll show you. I know you, Cyn. I know you better than you know yourself. I'm going to tug off your sweater again, and you're going to let me."

He's a liar, but he's not wrong. "You'll have to let go of either your knife or your cock to do that," I dare.

"My dick, then. But that's only because I'll need my knife in a second. And my dick? Well, baby, we both know that's yours. Give me a second, and I'll make sure to give it to you."

My pulse jumps. I try to keep my own expression neutral, but when it comes to Clay… I can't help myself. I've never been able to.

The only time our stare is broken is when he uses one hand to tug my sweater up and over my head.

His cock is still out, but he's ignoring it in favor of ogling my chest again.

Just to be a tease, I arch my back, giving him better access to my tits.

"Did you miss me?" Clay breathes out. Then, because I tempted him, he lifts the knife he's still holding. Using the bloody blade, he slices the front of my bra open. Brushing the cut cups out of his way with the back of his hand, the bra hangs by my pits as my bare tits are revealed to him. He squeezes one, and I clamp my thighs together as he purrs, "Did you touch yourself and think of me?"

I give him a look that says: Wouldn't you like to know?

He gets so close, his breath washes over me, warming me to my core. "When you let Tommy climb on top and fuck you, did you see my face?"

My lips part, readying to kiss him.

No.

I pull my head back.

Okay.

That's it. I let him have his fun. Covering my chest with my arms, I turn and give him my cheek instead.

"Clay, stop this. You were dead. Obviously you're not. It doesn't matter. You moved on."

"No, Cyn. *You did.*"

Something in his tone has my head snapping back toward him. His face is twisted. I open my mouth, but something—his expression, my *guilt*—has me closing it. My teeth *click*, and I shrug as he… he…

'Rages' is the only word I can think of to describe his reaction. Clay shoves his erection inside of his pants, doing up the zipper even though he leaves the button undone. He paces. Stomps. Glares.

And then he points the bloody knife at me.

"You and Tommy… he got to touch you. Taste you. *Fuck* you… and only when he was too busy fucking Summer Kaye did I even get his *scraps.*"

Talk about whiplash. I just killed a man, and I'm completely able to disregard that because Clay just said—

"When we were kids? I was with you then."

"No, Cyn," he erupts. "This whole last damn *year.*"

What?

"No. *No.* Tommy isn't cheating on me. Fucking *Summer?*" I remember those besotted looks, the way he insisted we be friends, how he's been so secretive lately… coming home late… There never was going to be a proposal, was there? No… "They had a fling when they were kids. That's all—"

"I saw them. Plenty of times. Hell, they were in a motel together just last week."

I shake my head.

"I didn't follow him often," adds Clay. "You were the one I was always compelled to keep my eye on, but that was easy. You stayed where he put you. Such a good girl sometimes, and so very wicked at others. But if I knew Tommy was getting some from Tyler's bitch of a wife, then it was fair that I got some from *mine.*"

"Wha— what are you saying?"

"That I never once for a moment haven't thought of you as my wife. I did what I had to do. Just like Tommy did—"

"He had to cheat on me? Is *that* what you're saying?"

"Yes." It's a simple enough answer that, like everything else, makes no fucking sense. "He did. He'll explain. I promise, Cyn, you'll understand—"

A bewildered sob rises up in my throat. "No, Clay. I don't think I'll ever be able to understand *any* of this. You leaving me. Tommy cheating on me. I promised him I would never do anything like that again, but *he* did?" My mouth works for a second, unable to find the words—

until I do. "Is this *my* punishment? I lost the love of my life and my second chance?"

Maybe death would've been better.

Clay's whole cocky attitude shifts. I know why, too. He heard it in my voice. The rejection. The pain.

If there's anyone who knows how badly I take to being rejected, it's Clayton Rivers—and he lunges for me.

I step back.

I don't even give a shit that my bra is ruined and that I'm standing here topless. I shrug it off, then hug myself.

He closes the gap between us, cradling my elbows in his hands. "Don't be upset, baby. I didn't tell you to make you upset. Tommy didn't pick Summer over you. You know that. He wouldn't do that. But she made him sneak around with her. Just like *I* made *you*. Does that make it better?"

This whole night's already been so absurd, why shouldn't I laugh at that? It's a hollow laugh, yes, but that's all I can muster at the moment. "What happened? Their clothes fell off, he tripped and landed dick-first into that stupid bitch? Is that what you want me to believe?"

Clay releases me, then tugs the front strands of his hair until they stand up on end. "*Fuck.* I messed up. He was doing it to protect you, to keep Summer's mouth shut for once and for all. If you knew, you wouldn't understand. You gotta believe me."

I can't. Not when he's spent five years lying to me.

Five? Who am I kidding? It's probably been *ten.*

"How do you know?" A sinking suspicion slams into me. He said that Chase didn't know that he was alive. Did Tommy? "That he was fucking another woman to *protect* me?"

"Don't worry about that."

"Clayton—"

He holds out his hand. How convenient. It's the one with his *knife*. "Let's make a deal. Okay? How 'bout that, Cyn? Until the night's over, I won't hold you cheating on me against you. You don't hold it against Tommy. And when the night's over—"

We'll all be dead, right?

My fury at this whole situation overpowers every other emotion I'm feeling right now.

"Why do you care?" I snap. I throw open my arms, tits bouncing, and it's a marvel that he's not distracted enough to ignore what I say next. "You're just going to kill him anyway! And me, too, I bet. Jesus Christ, Clay, why didn't you bleed me out before you faked your own death, huh? I don't even know why you did it. Honestly? I couldn't care less," I lie. "But death would've been preferable to living without you. You know that? So why not kill me now?"

Thunder flashes across his expression. "Never."

Look at that. Called his bluff. I think I always knew, from the moment he removed the mask, that of all of us on the island, I was the only one who might be safe.

From being slaughtered, that is. From everything else that Clay has in mind for me?

Not a chance.

I'm already half-naked. With a barely stifled roar, he yanks his cock back out. He's still hard, still wanting, and as he disappears his hand behind him, pulling out a fist full of *something*, I know that I haven't distracted him from getting what he wants at all.

"You're my wife, Cyn. You've always been mine. You hear me? *Mine*."

"If you felt that way, you shouldn't have left."

He advances on me again, so threatening that, if it was anyone *but* Clay, I'd be shitting myself out of pure terror. But it's Clay and, fucking hell, all I can think about is the salty taste he left on my lips, the come smeared on my neck, and how powerful I felt at that moment, slicing Clay right after he came.

He's no worse for the wear now. I know I got him, though except for the slice in his sweatshirt, you'd never know.

"Understand this. Wherever you've gone, I've followed. You were *never* alone. I was never far. But I did what I set out to do. I made it the five fucking years that cost me everything. My life. My sanity. My *wife*. But after tonight, I'll have that all back. And it starts with *you*."

If only I could believe that. His words are the ramblings of an obsessed stalker, a man so fixated on spending the rest of his life with me after he vanished on his own accord, he killed my high school tormentors—and now he's also trying to convince me to forgive my new boyfriend for cheating on me after believing I cheated on *Clay* with him.

Because they have a past, too?

None of this makes sense, and I don't think it will until I have the answer to one question.

"Why did you go, Clay?" My voice is barely a whisper. In the quiet of the woods, he hears me anyway. "Why did you leave me?"

Clay closes the gap between us again. Still holding his knife, he cradles my jaw in his hands. "I wouldn't have if I had any choice."

I'm risking getting sliced, but I barely even realize that as I use all of my strength to shove him away from me.

"You were gone! Dead! I buried an empty fucking casket, Clay! For more than two years, I waited for a sign that you survived because, damn it, I *knew* you weren't dead. In New Jersey, then in Gullhaven. I *waited.*"

"So did I. But I'm back—"

"And I've changed."

Clay holds out his hands, then slams his fists against his chest. "So have I, baby."

Don't I know it?

"The Clay I knew wasn't a murderer."

His face shadows over. "That Clay died the day I spilled my blood in that Audi and forced myself to walk away from my wife. And now… to get you back. To *keep* you… there isn't anyone I won't kill."

And, okay.

That does it.

I've just hit my breaking point.

Wow. All that therapy must've been worth it in the long run because my sanity lasted way longer than I thought before it just *shattered.*

For me… he wants me to believe he did this for me. When all he had to do was be my husband. Stay home with me. Fuck me. Buy me things, tell me I was pretty, tell me he loved me. He never would've lost me then, and now he's desperate to get me back?

I laugh, sounding as hysterical as Summer did. Then I remember she can't laugh because she doesn't have a tongue… that she can't laugh because *Clay killed her…* and my own laugh becomes crazed. "I can't fucking believe it. It's true. My 'dead' husband is now a spree killer."

He likes the sound of my laugh, crazed or not. His answering smile is a wicked one, and I hate myself that it's enough to have me ready to fucking crawl to him all over again. "I prefer 'serial'."

"Isn't a spree killer one who just kills at random with no time in between?" That's what happens when you wind down at bedtime, watching true crime TV. Shit like that sticks in your head, and it's so much easier to argue the definitions of the different types of killers than face the fact that I'm *married* to one. "Serial killers plan."

He smirks. "That's my point."

My laughter dies. Okay. It's not funny anymore. I don't think it ever was. "Clay—"

"You don't get it, baby. I've got the taste of blood now. If leaving bodies behind is a way to get you to understand how much I fucking love you, no one is safe." He's suddenly dead serious as he adds, "I can't exist without you."

My fingers clench into tight fists. "Oh? You made it just fine for five years."

There goes that wild look in his eyes again. "I was there. I was *always* there. You can't tell me you didn't sense my eyes on you."

For the second time, I open my mouth, think better of the answer, then close it.

Because, damn it, he's right. I *did*. I thought I was crazy. How I saw him lurking in the shadows, swore I felt his hands on my body, and smelled his familiar scent all around me…

He knows, too. Obviously.

He was *there*.

And he's done playing now, too.

"Take off your pants," he orders.

Don't think about that, Cyn. This is about survival. This is about winning this goddamn game between us. Making it to the end credits any way you can.

Questions later. Answers later.

Confessions from a man I would've thought pathologically loyal to me *later*…

But if this is some kind of game to my husband, he won't expect me to play along all that easily. So I give my head a royal shake and ask, "And if I don't?"

"You're my wife," is his response. "You gonna deny me? My wife? All I wanted was you… and I'm going to have you. So, please, for once… do what I said. Take off your jeans."

He won't hurt me if I don't. Despite how much control he's lost, I'm absolutely positive that, if I refused him, he'd rage and he'd threaten but he would never hold me down and force me to take him. Our relationship was built on sex and consent. I let him do whatever he wanted to me, whenever he wanted, but we both knew that's because he had my permission.

So when I take off my jeans? I don't do it because he told me to. I do it because I *want* to.

Because it's Clay?

Because the thought that Summer Kaye touched Tommy has me burning up with so much jealousy and anger that I can't make it simmer? That all I can do is get my tiny spark of revenge by pleasuring Clay and pretending like he forced me to or else I might be his next victim?

Summer is dead. Tommy might be. There's no way to know for sure until I see his crooked smile or his bloody body. Will letting Clay fuck me—fucking my husband—change the truth if Tommy really did stick his dick in my frenemy?

No.

But I'm going to do it anyway.

He sighs, the sound of relief so ragged, yet so beautiful. He strokes his cock as he advances on me once more.

With the exception of his dick being out, he's fully clothed. He makes no move to undress and, for some reason, that does something to the banked terror that's still lurking beneath the pain and the jealousy.

It disappears as sudden arousal has me leaning toward him on my own.

His lips twitch, a daring grin. "Did you miss me, Cyn?" he repeats.

I don't lie. Not to Clay, at least. He's the only one who loved me no matter my truth. Who would *never* cheat on me—

"Yes!"

He presses the bloody blade against my naked side. It's sticky and it's cold, and I *shiver* as he twists it enough to cut through the thin band on my thong.

"Then prove it."

The moment I let him stick his dick in my mouth, I knew I'd end up beneath him. But looks like I underestimated him because, as soon as he tosses the knife to the grass—thrown because, fuck it, he knows I'm not about to grab it and use it on him again—he opens up his folded fist and shows me what he pulled out of his pocket.

A condom—and a small travel-sized bottle of lubricant.

"On your knees. Until you tell me you're my wife again, you're my whore. So get back on your knees where you belong."

I swallow roughly. A combination of nerves and

undeniable arousal makes my throat feel thick. "You're not gonna do what I *think* you're gonna do, are you?"

Clay's tongue darts out, dabbing his bottom lip. He lifts an eyebrow. "You mean take you in the dirt as I fuck that tight asshole of yours? That's exactly what I'm gonna do." He tucks the bottle under his arm, freeing his hands so that he can pull on the condom. "Usually we have more time to prep. You're my wife. There should never be anything between us. But... I *need* this. I need *you*. So if it's take the same pussy you give to Tommy whenever he wants or fuck the ass that's only ever been mine? A condom will do tonight."

Once he's covered, he opens the bottle of lube. "I'd tell you to loosen up, but I think we both know that's not likely. I'll make sure to use enough of this stuff, though. Trust me, Cyn. I'll show you exactly why you missed me. Now get on your knees, or you can come here and ride me instead. I don't care how I take you so long as I get to *take* you."

Clay's right. When we were adventurous and newly married, I'd let him have anal whenever he wanted. But I would prep for it if I could tell he was in the mood, and I'd know it was coming so I'd be able to relax in time to make the experience pleasurable for both of us.

I prefer him to fuck my pussy, of course. It's more pleasure, less pain, because no matter how much lube he uses, the pressure is different. The sensation is different. I still liked it when he did it because it was *Clay*, but once I got with Tommy, I wasn't into it.

So tell me why, as I drop to my knees then fall over onto all fours, am I irrationally looking forward to him filling my ass with his cock?

Maybe it's because I recognize that look in Clay's eyes. Even before he obviously lost his mind, I could tell when he wouldn't be budged from something. All that talk before about whether or not I gave Tommy all of me… he knows I didn't, and now, if only to prove to himself that he has some kind of claim after all these years, he wants to do this.

And he will. He'll stop short of forcing me to because of the damage he could inflict, but we both know how I've always been putty in his hands. If he wanted, all he'd have to do is give me head or fuck my pussy first, then my ass would be his anyway.

But as he crouches down, slathering my backside with enough lube to have me shivering from the unexpected chill against my overheated skin, I can tell that desperation has won out. He needs to do this, and he needs to do this *now*.

WELCOME TO
HALO ISLAND
'til death
do we part...

SIXTEEN
TOMMY, NO

I guess I should be grateful that he tests the puckered skin with his thumb first. It burns as he forces the digit past the tight inner rim of skin, but after he prods and stretches and adds just a touch more lube, he seems satisfied.

I'm keening beneath him as he mounts me.

"Relax, Cyn," he murmurs, replacing his thumb with the head of his cock. "It'll feel so much better if you relax."

"I have a killer fucking my ass," I snap. "You relax."

He laughs. The insane fucker *laughs.* "No," he says, pushing the head inside of me, pausing when I tighten up at the intrusive sensation. "You have your husband fucking your ass. Remember that, baby. I'm your husband, and it's not even your ass. Not really. It's *mine.*"

Another inch. I take a shallow breath, breathing

through the discomfort. It won't last. It never did. When Clay first worked his dick inside of me like this, I could never escape feeling like I was going to burst. He would take his time, making it easy for me, and eventually the uncomfortable fullness faded to something closer to pleasure.

And if I needed a little help relaxing? Clay would reach around me, find my clit, and rub it until I was so distracted by the sense of coming, I barely noticed that he was rocking into my ass, fucking me with short, shallow thrusts.

They don't have to be full ones. Clay used to tell me my ass was so tight, just a few pumps were enough to have him shooting his load inside of me. That's why I put up with it. He wouldn't last long, and my grateful husband would spend the next hour eating my ass, eating my pussy, giving me as many orgasms as I wanted as a thank you for letting him have me like that.

I don't expect the same treatment now. I'm almost sure that he decided to fuck my ass out in the open as another punishment for moving on with Tommy. Hell, he probably wishes that Tommy was the one I was forced to kill so that he could have sex with me next to my most recent lover's body.

A lover who *cheated* on me.

I can't forget that. I don't know if it's true. Clay's already proven himself to be a liar. That could be another lie, but part of me senses that it *is* true. Tommy cheated on me. Doesn't matter that I did it first, or that—technically—I'm doing it again right this very second as Clay slowly pushes himself into my ass.

When I think of Tommy and Summer together? I have to do something, and that something is Clayton Rivers.

So I rear back, taking as much of Clay as I can. I scream. I don't know why. It hurts, but I'm used to pain. It feels too intense, but I don't care about that. I scream because I want to, just like I wanted to fuck Clay.

And now he's fucking me.

"Oh, Cyn." He braces his arms on both sides of me, his sweatshirt rubbing against my back as he moves. "My perfect whore. My good, good girl. My fucking amazing wife. I thought I imagined how good you felt, wrapped around my cock like this. I can't wait until I can lose the condom and have you hugging my cock again. This… this right here? It was worth the wait. It was worth the *blood.*"

I'm glad he thinks so.

He ducks his head, burying his nose in my loose hair. "I promise. I'll make it up to you. I'm back. I'm not going anywhere. Nothing… *no one…* will separate us again. You understand me?"

I do.

Do I believe him?

That's a trickier question.

When I don't answer, he actually does reach around me. He finds my clit, playing with it like it's his favorite toy, and even if I wanted to deny him giving me an orgasm like this, my traitorous body has other ideas.

I scream again, but this one is pure pleasure. My legs go weak. My nails dig in the dirt as I ride out my climax, all while Clay refuses to release my clit until I finally collapse beneath him and he moves his hand to alter his angle a little. He's still fucking me, but it doesn't last. Two more pumps and Clay fists the grass, grunting through clenched teeth as he finishes inside of me.

Only then, when he's done, does he let his weight settle on my back, keeping me trapped beneath him.

Somehow, we ended up by the knife. He grabs it, wiping as much of the blood off of it on the grass as he can. Once he's pleased with the blade, he moves it in front of me, our reflections staring back at us.

I look well-fucked. Clay looks well-pleased.

He grins. "Oh, yeah, baby. You understand very well, don't you?"

I DON'T KNOW WHAT'S WORSE: THAT CLAY TIES UP THE used condom and pockets it, or he gets on his knees behind me, plugging my sore asshole as he checks to make sure he didn't do any damage while he was fucking me.

Without the lube, he would've torn me in half. Even with the lube, he could barely thrust, I was that tight. The sex act wasn't about pleasure. He made sure I got mine whether I wanted it or not, and he sure as hell got his as evidenced by the load in the condom, but I know better. It was an act of possession, and now that Clay's proved to himself that I'll still give in to him even after all this time, something about him... shifts.

He changes.

I see a glimpse of the man I married in the way he assures himself that I'm in as good a shape as can be expected after killing Chase, then being fucked in the ass next to his corpse. Clay palms my ass cheek, dropping a kiss to the small of my back, then gets to his feet.

He finds my clothes. My panties go in another pocket. He leaves my ruined bra behind, then helps me pull on my jeans before easing my blood-stained sweater over my head. I give no resistance as he threads one arm through, then the next, until I'm covered.

Clay disappears his knife back into its sheath. I never for a moment forget that it's there, and that's the main reason I allow him to curve my hand around his shoulder as he tilts me back, lifting me in a bridal-style carry.

We abandon my shoes with Chase. Because it's easier to focus on ridiculous bullshit instead of the very real fact that my husband's returned from the dead as a psychotic murderer, I'm grateful I have another pair of sneakers back at the cabin. When I run again... because I *will* run again if given the chance... at least I won't be barefoot.

I'm not exactly a lightweight, but Clay absolutely refuses to put me down again until he's brought me to the cabin I've shared with Tommy these last couple of days.

Only then does he return me to my feet, never once giving any sign that he struggled to carry me all this way as he uses the key he somehow managed to steal from Tommy to let us in.

Closing the door behind him, he jerks his head at the couch. It's halfway in the middle of the front room, most likely from when Clay used the key to let himself in before he chased me out through the back door.

"Go on, Cyn. Take a seat. Get comfy."

"Why?" I ask, even as I drop down on the couch. My fingers are trembling nervously. I fist them before Clay can notice. "What are we doing?"

What is *he* doing?

He takes up a position near the front door. Crossing his ankles as he leans back against the wall, Clay crosses his arms over his chest next. His knife is out again, and the expression on his face would be irresistible if it wasn't for what he says to me once he's in position.

"What are we doing?" he echoes. "We're waiting for Tommy."

No. "You said you wouldn't hurt him. If I—"

He clicks his tongue. "No. I believe I asked you what you would give me if I spared him. I didn't make any promises, Cyn. Not like you did when you vowed to be mine, for better or for worse."

Anger makes me hot. It makes me *reckless*. "I guess this is the 'worse' part then, huh, Clay?"

He shrugs. "If that's what you want to think. It

doesn't matter anyway. The night's not over yet." With a smirk, he adds, "Let's see how much worse it can get."

TIME CRAWLS. EVERY SECOND ON THAT COUCH IS AN eternity as I listen for any sound that Tommy's approaching.

If I can believe Clay, he's not dead yet. It would be the most fucked-up thing he did all night if he lied, telling me we're waiting for Tommy when, in reality, he'd dead somewhere on Halo Island. I have hope that Tommy is okay, hope that he'll survive until morning and get to the ferry instead of returning to the cabin.

But I know better. If there's any chance that I survived the masked killer on the island, he'll come looking for me. He'll have to check the cabin. He'll come through the front door, and he'll be killed without even having the chance to protect himself if Clay attacks him.

Tommy obviously can protect himself otherwise. With everything else that has happened, I haven't been able to really come to terms with the fact that Tommy is *also* a killer. It doesn't matter that Chase didn't die from his injuries, or that I had to show mercy and finish him off after Clay insisted. Tommy used the cover of Clay's insanity to get revenge on the boy who hurt me a decade ago. He had to have thought that, when Clay was caught, he could blame Chase's murder on him.

But that's assuming he survives Clay first...

He's whistling. Twisting his knife, whistling a song I know to the marrow of my bones—*Stand by Me* by Ben E. King, our unofficial wedding song after we eloped—he goes from watching me with a possessive stare to peeking out the window, searching for his last victim.

And then, about a half an hour after we returned to the cabin, everything shifts again. A sense of anticipation creeps into the room as Clay moves away from the window, resuming his position on the other side of the door, ready to spring out again.

Clay's green eyes twinkle madly as he puts his finger to his lips, the flat of his blade against his cheek. "Shh, babe. We don't want to ruin the surprise."

I freeze, mind racing as I try to figure out how to get Tommy away from here before Clay confronts him.

Confronts him, I think, hysterical and terrified. No. *Kills* him. He's going to *kill* him.

But he won't kill me. I'm sure about that now. He was bluffing before, threatening my life so that I could feel justified in obeying his commands to get on my knees and suck him off. And if part of me just wanted to crawl to him because he *is*—*was*—my husband, I refuse to examine that too closely, not when I'm going to be responsible for *another* death.

I actually care about this one. And if that makes me terrible to admit it, I don't give a shit. If Tommy's only crime was loving me, that's not enough to sit here quietly while Clay plots to murder his former best friend.

And that's why, the second the unlocked knob begins to turn, I take a deep breath and shout, "Tommy, no!"

I'm too late.

The door pulls outward. Tommy… Tommy fucking Gillis… with his handsome face and those beautiful curls and the eyes that have always been so loving, so *kind*… Tommy walks into the cabin, lips splitting into a relieved smile when he sees me sitting on the small couch in the middle of the front room.

Clay steps out from his hiding spot, his knife high.

Tommy goes still.

I sob, but I'm frozen in place. I can't stop what's about to happen. I can't even find the nerve to get up from the couch. I'm stuck, and I watch helplessly as Clay's arm moves.

But the knife never lands. Clay turns the point of the blade inward, angling it away from Tommy as he throws one arm around his shoulder, an awkward one-sided hug. With his other hand, Clay clasps Tommy's in his as he pats Tommy on the back in welcome.

My mouth falls open as my heart just about *stops*.

"Fucking hell, man? What took you so long? We've been waiting."

What?

Tommy claps Clay on the back in return, then backs away. He ruffles his hand through his sweat-damped curls, the heights of his cheeks redder than usual. "I know. Sorry. I circled back to make sure that we got everyone."

What?

"I know. You left Chase alive."

Tommy shrugs, the gesture so impish and, well, *Tommy*, that I know it's *my* Tommy despite all other evidence to the contrary. "Yeah, I know. Sorry. I know it went against what I was supposed to do, but fuck me, Clay. Even when I forced him to spill his guts, he still insisted that Cyn came onto him that night. He needed to suffer."

"I figured. That's okay. He's dead now."

"I saw." Tommy points his finger at Clay. "Nice work. You're a natural with a knife."

"Guns are too easy," Clay answers, and I can't shake the feeling that I've somehow left Halo Island, transported back to that weirdo bizarro world instead. Or a horror movie. This is a B-rated slasher film with an ending that *makes no fucking sense.*

And then he says, "Besides, after all the planning we did for tonight, I wanted the kills to be up close and personal. They all deserved that. But Chase… that wasn't me. Cyn got to finish him off."

Tommy's eyes widen, turning to me. Relief flashes across his face. "So she understands. She gets it."

No, the fuck I *don't.*

Planning?

I'm so lost. So damn confused, too, and it's obvious.

That's not the only thing that is, either.

"Cyn? Love?" My stomach revolts as he uses that pet name for me. "What's the matter?"

What's the matter? What's the *matter*?

"You… him… you *knew* about this? About all of this? You were *part* of it?"

The murders… I thought Tommy took advantage of what Clay was doing. I was wrong. He didn't kill Chase on a whim. Oh, no. This shit was planned.

Why? How?

What?

Tommy's brow furrows. With a frown, he cocks his head at Clay. "You didn't tell her."

"Tell me what?" I demand.

Clay sheathes his knife, a further clue that I got it *way* wrong when I thought he was going to kill Tommy next. "I was waiting for you. If it came from me, she wouldn't believe it. She'd think I was lying."

I get to my feet. "Because you're a liar," I accuse.

He thins his lips. "I did what I had to. Right, Tommy?"

To my horror, Tommy nods. "Don't blame Clay, Cyn. He was just following the plan."

"Plan," I echo. "What fucking plan?"

Tommy gentles his voice. "Why don't you sit down. It'll be easier to explain if you're relaxed."

A shitload of Xanax couldn't relax me right now. "I'm good. Now tell me what the hell is going on."

"You know most of it already," Clay says. As an aside to Tommy, he explains, "I told her why Vee had to die. How Tyler needed to go because of Summer. How I had fun with offing that bitch, and Aaron… well, just because we bought the island, that doesn't mean I could sneak on without my own ferry." He glances at Tommy. "Maybe we should've gotten a ferry. Ah. Next time."

I blink, trying to make sense of what he just said. "You… you bought the island?"

"Sure did. Through an LLC I set up before I had to fake my death. It was Tommy's idea. Actually, everything was Tommy's idea. But the island especially. We know how much it means to you, babe. If we were going to show you how far we were willing to go to make you ours, it needed to be here. Everything started on Halo Island. It's only fair it ends here, too."

"Right," adds Tommy. "Because the lives we had are finished. We're starting over now. You. Me. Clay. Just like it should've always been."

"Don't be worried if this is all too much. Believe me, it took years for Tommy to convince me this was the right thing to do. That it wasn't fair that he had you first, and I stole you. So we made an agreement. I got you for five years. Seventeen to twenty-two. With me out of the picture, he got the next five years to make you love him. Then, once you did, I get to come back and we both get you for the rest of our lives."

"You love me," Tommy says. It's strange, though. His words are soft. Gentle. But they ring with steel. "I know you do. Just in time, too. This Halloween… I was going to make this anniversary of Clay's death one you'll never forget." He grins that crooked grin. "By letting you know that he was still alive, waiting to return to you."

So he did know. He knew all along that Clay was alive.

I can't believe this. I *mourned* him. I cried on Tommy's shoulder. We were the only two fucking people when I buried that empty casket, and he *knew*?

They *planned* this?

Well, at least I know how Clay got the cabin key from Tommy without having to kill him first.

WELCOME TO
HALO ISLAND
'til death
do we part...

SEVENTEEN

EVERYTHING

Clay answers all of my unasked questions without me even having to ask them at all when he says, "We planned everything, babe. From bleeding myself enough to store up a supply to splash over the car to arranging for Tommy to convince you to move back to Gullhaven… buying the island. Inviting everyone who's ever hurt you to it. Killing them off one by one—"

"I got to kill Madison," Tommy cuts in proudly. "Clay helped me string her up after he was done with Summer—"

"Had to make her look like a puppet," interrupts Clay. "After all, when Madison opened her mouth, Summer's voice came out."

Tommy nods. "That's right. But I want you to know that I wasn't afraid of killing for you, either, Cyn. I would do *anything* for you."

Clay casts a side-long look at Tommy. "Except kill Summer. You made me do that."

Tommy's nostrils flare, his cheeks going hollow. "We had a plan, Clay. I lured the girls out. You grabbed one. I grabbed one. It didn't matter who. It just had to be done."

"True," Clay admits. "And, to be fucking honest, I wanted a shot at Summer. No one blackmails my wife and my pal and gets away with it." He turns his attention back on me. "We've both always known we'd do anything for you, and now we've proven it, baby. You always want proof. You always needed to *see* that someone cared about you. Well, this is it. I sacrificed five years without my wife to give you a chance to find happiness with Tommy. He let me take you with me to New Jersey in the first place. And now it's time we get what we worked so hard for so long for."

There's something about the way these two murderers are staring at me now that has me seconds away from turning from them, bolting through the back again, and taking my chances in the woods.

Silly Cyn. You should've known better than to run from your husband…

Clay will chase me. Now I know that Tommy will, too. Nothing will stop them from getting what they want.

And, fucking hell, they want *me*.

But I play dumb. I pretend I don't know what they're talking about. Gulping, I say in a ragged voice, "And what is that?"

"We get to share you."

"Share me?" Like the three of us play house or something? We put the murders on Halo Island behind us, vanish far away from Gullhaven, then I become a bigamist? Share? I… I don't share. "Clay, this is insane. Both of you, stay away from me."

"Oh, Cyn. You know better than to think I can ever do that. Even when I was 'dead', I was there. Told you. I'll *always* be there. I'm a part of you now and forever. And Tommy will be, too. Won't you, Tommy?"

"I love you," he gasps. *Pleads.* "I did this because I love you. Please tell me you love me back."

I can't. Not right now.

Not when I'm coming to terms with the fact that everything that we had—everything I thought I knew—was a lie.

I thought Clay broke my heart anew earlier tonight when he admitted that Tommy and Summer were having an affair. I can't even bring myself to confront Tommy about that, and hearing that Clay left me all those years ago because his best friend told him to…

Wait.

They want to share me. They want to be a *part* of me.

They—

"Share me?" I ask. "What the fuck do you mean?"

Clay's hand dips into his pocket. When he pulls out that small bottle of lube from before, I know *exactly* what he means.

I hold up my hands. "No."

"No?" echoes Clay. His lips twitch, amused. "You going to deny your husband? Your lover? You never have before."

His free hand ghosts over his pocket. I know what's in there. The dirty, used condom is stashed inside like some kind of fucking trophy.

"You're sick," I spit at him again. "I already gave you what you wanted, Clay. Now you want *more*?"

His eyes flash. "I want *everything*."

I know. He confessed as much as he was carrying me back to the cabin.

That's why he snuck into my bed and fucked me, purposely letting me believe that it was Tommy who came all over me. When Clay first admitted that to me after he had my ass, it was something else that didn't make sense. I mean, I believed him. Part of me knew instinctively that the man with the husky voice and the possessive touch had to have been my husband. Once I knew the truth, that he was *alive*, I subconsciously knew it was him.

But Tommy…

Summer is dead, yet I still can't bring myself to regret one of our last exchanges. She thought she could accuse me of murder, and I responded by throwing it in her face that my alibi revolved around Tommy and me fucking. I remember how pissed she looked, and I thought it was because she hated how I one-upped her. Of course, now I know it's because she was blackmailing *my* boyfriend into fucking her on the regular. If Tommy and Clay were working together toward murder, just like Billy Loomis and Stu Macher, maybe that night was all part of the plan.

Clay got his chance to have sex with me before I learned the truth while Tommy was… what? Fucking Summer? There's no denying that they were together, supposedly searching for Tyler and Vee, but was that what they were really doing? Tommy wasn't with me, though, and when I threw it in Summer's face that I thought he *was*, he never reacted. He went along with it instead of being confused that I was covered in come like I claimed, but it wasn't his.

Did he think I was making it up to annoy Summer? Or did he keep from reacting because he already *knew* that Clayton Rivers fucked me while he was indisposed?

Is that why he wants to fuck me now?

Everything about Tommy changed the moment Clay pulled out the bottle of lube. Before, he was careful, letting Clay explain their grand plan, ducking his head a little when Clay confessed that this was all Tommy's initial idea, that he's spent ten years plotting a way to get me back in his life for good.

Because he couldn't be without me. Because he managed to convince Clay that, even while I wear his ring, Tommy had the prior claim to me. Like he 'called' me by being my first fuck, my first love, and he'd rather take his turn however he could than know I'd never be with him.

But Clay… he was my *husband*. He won. He pursued

me; he did every dirty trick in the book he could when we were kids to convince me to choose him over Tommy. For fuck's sake, we had a full-blown affair for months before I finally confessed to my high school sweetheart that I was running away to New Jersey with his best friend… Clay would lose it whenever another guy paid me any attention, but he's willing to share me with Tommy?

And that's why, I realize as Tommy watches me with an expression of desire, need, and fucking *hope*. It's not just some guy. It's Tommy, and though I'm clearly still technically married since Clay's alive, I don't think I was that far off-base when I suspected he was going to propose to me during our stay on the island.

Both of these men want forever. They want it so badly that they've *killed* in order to get it, and now that they've laid their offer at my feet, they expect me to sacrifice myself to them next.

Only I'm not their next victim. I'm the final girl in this slasher film. I've survived, and my prize for making it to the end of this horror movie is the two killers taking their turns fucking me.

No. I see the expectant look on Clay's face as he gives the bottle of lube a little shake. I see the hunger on Tommy's. Clay's not-too-subtle gesture toward his pocket. The way Tommy is prowling slightly, his body coiled, everything about him telling me he's ready to pounce.

I glare at Clay. "Damn it, Clay. You really are a sick fuck, aren't you? You didn't fuck me in the ass because you knew that's something I've only ever done with you. You did it because you planned on doing it again in front of Tommy and wanted to make sure I was ready."

Tommy winces. Looks like I hit a sore spot when I mentioned *my* newly sore spot. For all their talk of making this a threesome where both of the guys are devoted to me, Tommy is as jealous as Clay is. He asked me once for anal, I flatly refused, and he never mentioned it again.

Now he knows why, and I make a note of how he reacts.

They think they own me. They think I'll just listen and do what they want because they *killed* for me.

We'll see about that.

Clay doesn't even deny my accusations. "You're mostly right, Cyn. I love your pussy, but that ass is mine. Some things should be saved for your husband." He growls out the word, making it even more obvious that Clay thinks the title means something extra to him. That it's something else that Tommy can't claim… "But I don't plan on just fucking your ass in front of Tommy. There'll be plenty of time for that once we're off this goddamn island. But tonight? We're going to show you what it took us too fucking long to accept. You belong to both of us. That means you're going to *fuck* both of us." He twists the cap off the lube. "At the same time."

My traitorous pussy clenches as I instantly imagine what it would be like to have both Clay and Tommy inside of me together.

I could do it. I'm pretty confident I can. Maybe if Clay hadn't already shoved his thick cock into my ass tonight—or he didn't have that bottle of lube handy—I'd be looking for a way to get past these two guys before they fucked me in half. If they were careful not to hurt me, I think I could take them both at the same time... I've just never thought I ever would.

Fuck. *Fuck.* Is this my punishment or another 'gift' from my husband? I loved Clay with everything I had. More than that, I trusted him with all the secret, dark parts of me that not even Tommy's ever seen.

This isn't just their twisted fantasy come true. It's also *mine*.

I mentioned it to Clay once. When we were first fucking like bunnies all over his empty house, exploring each other, exploring our sexualities... I asked him if we could bring Tommy into our game. That's what it was. Before I loved him, I was so incredibly sexually combustible with him, I would've burned even without his damn touch.

His reaction still haunts me to this day. He swore, if I ever fucked another man—even Tommy—that he'd kill him, then himself. Not me. Never me. But he couldn't live with knowing that I ever wanted anyone more than I wanted him.

When he died, I wondered. It was all so... staged. That's what confused the Little Falls police. Enough blood to make it obvious he couldn't survive, his car hidden but not really, the ID and phone left behind so they could figure out who their victim was… but no body. No motive. Just a missing man who never really was missing at all.

I never cheated again. I know they say that once a cheater, always a cheater, but Clay was it for me. If I can believe him, I was it for him.

And now, all these years later, he's finally invited Tommy into our game. Because of his own regrets? Or because he's trying to give me everything I wanted back then to make up for walking away five years ago?

They planned this. Clay watched me from the shadows, and Tommy was always there, so even if I did want to find another guy, they wouldn't have let me. And to prove that they mean it when they say that they've come to this agreement to share me, Clay's offering me the one thing I asked for way back then: a threesome with both of the men I loved.

And I'm such a glutton for punishment that I'm suddenly so aroused, I *hurt*.

Tommy takes a hesitant step toward me. He sees the look of pain twisting my face and gets the totally wrong idea. He thinks I'm rejecting him when, God fucking damn it, I'm already imagining him thrusting inside of me as Clay works his cock back into my ass.

And then Tommy gives me that old puppy-dog look, like he's begging at my feet, waiting to see if he'll get a treat… or get kicked. "Cyn. I… Listen. If you don't want to be with me… if you can't now that you know the truth—"

Fury replaces the want and need rushing through my veins. Thanks, Tommy. I needed the reminder that you're a liar, just like my husband.

"Which truth?" I ask, turning my venom on him. "That you've been fucking Summer behind my back? Or that you knew my husband was alive and never told me?"

Because now that I know they planned this… how can I trust either of them again?

Tommy's eyes go wild. "She knew, Cyn. I don't know how she found out. Only Clay and me were supposed to know. She would've told—"

And that *excuses* it?

"I don't care. You cheated on me." Hypocritical Cyn, but I don't give a shit. "You said you loved me, and you were with *her*."

Tommy sends a killing look at Clay. My husband shrugs as if to say that this is Tommy's shit show, even if Clay *is* the one who told me about Tommy and Summer.

He grits his teeth. "I wore a condom every time. I scrubbed her off of me. I never came home to you with her on me, Cyn. I fucking swear it. It was like using a damn fleshlight. That's how much she meant to me. It was only about ten times total once she told me how she knew. That's it. I would've killed her then, but…"

Clay cuts in: "It wasn't the plan."

I'm so sick and fucking tired of hearing about this plan.

What about *my* plans?

My life?

My happy ending?

When I don't say anything in response, Tommy surges forward, taking my head in his hands, forcing me to see the sincerity—and the insanity as clear as Clay's—in his deep blue eyes.

"You're the only one who matters to me. Who ever has. There isn't anything I won't do for you."

Including Summer fucking Kaye.

"Did you fuck her on the island?" I whisper.

"Cyn?"

I thought it was so strange how I kept waking up to Tommy being missing from our bed in the cabin. Add that to Summer's insistence that she spent the night in an empty one because she had to get away from Tyler's snoring, and how much do you want to bet that was just an excuse for Tommy and Summer to enjoy themselves while Clay took care of Tyler?

But then Tommy shakes his head with such force, mine follows along with it. "What? No. Why do you think she was so bitchy the whole time? She kept trying to sneak away from Tyler for a quickie, but I couldn't even fake it. Not when I was so close to getting rid of her for once and for all."

Jerking out of Tommy's hold, I search for Clay.

He holds up his hands, careful not to spill the lube. "I didn't see what they were doing, babe. Remember? I was too busy fucking *you*."

Tommy winces again. I glare at Clay. "I thought you were Tommy."

Clay's answering grin is cocky. "Did you really?"

He's not going to get me to admit that, half-asleep, when it was over—maybe in the middle of it—I fantasized that it was Clay. Because I knew? Because, somehow, I sensed that the man fucking me was my husband, not my boyfriend?

"It doesn't matter—"

"Oh, Cyn, but it *does*. You see, Tommy is so wound up, poor guy's going to fucking explode. He wouldn't let Summer touch him. And you... well, you thought you already did. But the truth is that Tommy hasn't gotten laid since we've been on the island together. You've spent the last two years with him. I've watched you together, biding my time, waiting my turn. He's twenty-eight. Prime of his fucking life. You think he can go days without getting off when he has such a tempting girlfriend as Cynthia Rivers?"

Oh, Clay. If he really has been watching me, we both know damn well that I dropped his name after I accepted he was gone. I'm Cynthia Preston, and I *was* Tommy's girlfriend... and now I don't know who or what I am anymore.

Halo Island has a habit of stealing from me. Now I feel like I've lost the core of who I was even as Clay watches me, waiting for me to deny everything else he just said.

When I don't, his expression turns to one of triumph. He nods at Tommy. "Drop your pants. Take out your cock. Let her see."

Not even an ounce of hesitation about removing his pants in front of Clay. Tommy unbuttons his jeans, unzips, then shoves both his pants and his boxer briefs down past his ass.

As his erection springs free, hard and stiff and weeping at the tip, Clay nods in approval, and Tommy's eyes return to me.

From the second they admitted they were in on this whole thing together, I couldn't help but wonder who the truly dominant partner was. The mastermind. The one in complete control over the other.

Growing up, they seemed so equal. If anything, Tommy was the more outgoing of the two. I know now that Clay seemed more inclined to lurk in his shadow because he was obsessing over the fact that Tommy had something he wanted. And once Clay had it, Tommy didn't give up. He *planned* this. He used his lifelong influence over Clay to convince him that they each get a turn to love me, and once I couldn't resist either of them any longer, we'd live happily fucking ever after together.

But when it comes to sex, Clay has something Tommy doesn't: his ring on my finger. That gives him an edge, and he runs with it as he reaches into his back pocket, pulling out another condom.

Just one, I notice. And though Tommy is the one with the obvious erection, he doesn't hand it to him.

Instead, Clay moves behind me. He lays his hand on the back of my neck, maneuvering my head until I have no choice but to take in Tommy's need for me.

"Look at him," he grates. "Look at how desperate he is for you."

Clay trails his hand down my back, the condom wrapper between his fingers rustling as he does. When he reaches the waistband of my dirty jeans, he slips his hand beneath it. Without any panties to stop him, his finger deftly caresses my puckered asshole. I stifle my moan, but it's too late. His husky chuckle on my skin tells me he heard it.

He shoves his hand further into my pants. It's his turn to groan now when he discovers how wet I am. "Tommy," he says. "Get on the bed."

Tommy doesn't hesitate. He quickly shucks his clothes, then climbs onto the bed. His back against the pillows, he strokes his cock, waiting for what's next.

I know what's next, even before Clay waves his free hand at me. "Go on, baby. Don't keep him like that. You wouldn't want him to get blue balls."

I scoff at Clay. "That might've worked on me when I was seventeen, dickhead. I know better now."

And, yet, I'm already padding toward the bed now that he's reluctantly drawn his hand back out of my jeans.

Tommy holds onto his cock, his gaze imploring me once more. "You don't have to do this," he tries again.

Oh. I know. I don't *have* to do anything.

But as I lift my sweater up and over my head, I admit if only for tonight: I *want* to.

"That's my girl," Clay murmurs, voice as proud as

Tommy's when he confessed he was responsible for Madison's murder. "Now go on. Spread that pussy for Tommy. Show us both what you have that was worth corrupting such a good man."

Tommy gulps, patting the bed next to him.

Good man? He's a murderer. They *both* are.

And that's still not going to stop me.

WELCOME TO
HALO ISLAND
'til death
do we part...

EIGHTEEN

TOGETHER

Once I'm completely naked, I climb onto the bed. Tommy's cock twitches in anticipation. I purposely refuse to look at either his face or Clay's as I throw one leg over him, grabbing his bare cock, and lodging it at my entrance.

For a split second, I wonder if I should ask for a condom. Now that I know about Summer… I should. After all, I know Clay has them. He only ever bought them for when I offered to let him fuck my ass, and the second he pulled that first one out, I knew what was going to happen.

To make Tommy wrap up would be a slap in the face. He did it with Summer, but we rarely used that layer of protection between us.

That seals it. Tomorrow might be different, but for now? I start to take him inside my soaked pussy.

"Yes… God *yes*." His hands land on my bare hips,

squeezing my flesh, angling me to take him as deep as possible. "I killed for you. I'll kill again. Anything. For this… there isn't anything I won't do."

I'll remember that.

As I sink on top of Tommy, I finally do look for Clay. He must have partially undressed while Tommy was positioning me right where he wanted me. He's half-naked, wearing a black t-shirt and nothing else, but with his pants gone, I can see he's just as fucking hard as Tommy. I stare at his cock for a second, unconsciously squeezing Tommy as I remember what it was like to have Clay fucking my ass… what? An hour ago?

Has my whole goddamn life changed in an *hour*?

Tommy lifts his hips, burying his cock impossibly deeper. I feel it since I'm still ogling Clay's sculpted body, the V on his hips where his shirt is riding up, and the cock jutting out from the junction of his legs, and, damn it, it feels *amazing*.

I'm not looking at my husband's face, though I hear the satisfaction in his voice as he says, "What a good girl. You took Tommy so well. Look at him. Like he's about to nut already. Don't you fucking do it, though, Tommy. Let her squeeze you. Let her fuck you. But don't you come until I join you. You got me?"

Tommy's voice is strangled. Because I tightened my core, squeezing him again? "I'm trying, Clay. But you know how good it feels inside of Cyn."

"Oh, I know. Why do you think I made sure to sneak in over the years and fuck her while you were busy?"

Clay chuckles. "She was still my wife, Tommy. Did you really think I'd go five years without fucking her?"

"No," he gasps. "Why the hell do you think I left the backdoor unlocked? She's yours. But, damn it—" He angles his hips enough to withdraw slightly, then slam up into me so hard that I bounce, "—she's mine, too."

I moan again. No matter how I feel about these two guys, or the sudden knowledge that they've been passing me back and forth for years, I can't help but react to the way that Tommy's fucking me. He knows how to work my body almost as well as Clay does, which is probably why I could never tell the difference between when one would take me or the other.

Do I care that they shared? I must be as twisted and damaged as they are because… I don't. It was just sex, and these are the only two I've ever had it with. They each have a claim to my body that I won't deny—otherwise I wouldn't be riding Tommy Gillis right now—but that's not what gives this a taste of hate sex.

They lied to me. Betrayed me.

And, one way or another, they're going to pay.

As I have that thought, I run my gaze over Clay again even as his best friend eases his thrusts, careful not to come too soon. My husband *preens*, and I firm my resolve. I'll admit that I enjoy the sight of his half-naked body way more than I should, but a quick flicker toward the floor reveals his pile of clothes—including his sheathed knife—not too far from the edge of the bed.

Then I see the torn remains of the condom packet

suddenly fluttering next to them and snap my head back up.

With the bottle of lube palmed in his hand, Clay uses four fingers to slip the condom on the bulbous head of his cock before rolling it up his length. He pours a liberal amount of the lube into his palm, slathering it on the condom, getting good and slick.

His eyes find mine as he pours more of the lubricant onto his hand before setting the bottle on the nightstand.

Prowling toward the bed, his covered cock leading the way, he smiles at me before putting a knee on the mattress.

Tommy picks up his pace even as Clay uses his clean hand to press down on my upper back, pushing my tits against Tommy's bare chest.

It's a new angle for him to penetrate me. He hits just the right nerves with his next thrust, and I mewl against his skin before lapping at the space between his pecs.

"Cyn," he pants softly. "Oh my fucking God, *yes*." His strokes become shallower as if desperate to keep pumping into me—or because he knows that, in a moment, I'll be so stuffed, he'll barely be able to move.

Because once my ass is in the air, Clay makes sure it's slick with lube before he climbs behind me and positions his cock against the rim of my asshole.

I know what to expect this time. I won't lie and say that there isn't a burn as he breaches me, but the feeling of him working the first inch or two of his cock into me while I'm full of Tommy in my pussy… I can handle the burn. I can handle the pain.

Fucking hell, I can handle both my husband and my lover.

He pushes a little harder as the weight of his body presses me further against Tommy.

I'm sprawled between them, my legs open, leaving them to fill me completely as Clay says between obviously gritted teeth, "I spent two fucking years watching Tommy have sex with you, Cyn, and that was after three of 'em, waiting for you to eventually welcome someone else into your bed, knowing if it was anyone other than him, I'd gut them. Then, when Tommy wasn't there, I took his place because I knew you needed me. You *craved* me." Yes. Damnit, *yes*. "I wanted to watch with you knowing I was there. To beg me to join you… but I should've known better about that one. If I want you, I have to take you. And, my pretty little wife, you're not going to stop me, are you?"

In answer, I arch my back just enough to take a little more of Clay.

"Ah, *yes*. That's my good girl. Take your husband's cock. I have more to give, baby, and you're going to take it all."

Tommy's stopped moving beneath me. He's still inside of me, but I'm stretched so tight, he has to be able to feel the girth of Clay's cock pressing down against him. Fuck. With as much of my husband as I've taken already, there's nowhere for either of them to go.

I thought I could handle them. Maybe… maybe I was wrong about that, too.

"I'm too full," I tell him. Full? Try *impaled*. "That's… that's enough."

"Silly Cyn," he says, and before I can do anything else, he brings down his hand, slapping me on the ass. I jump at the stinging sensation, and I don't know how it's possible, but he bottoms out inside of my ass. "See? That's my wife. You've had enough when I say you've had enough."

I gasp. "I fucking hate you."

He presses a kiss to my back. "Baby, if I believed you meant that, I'd kill myself for real. But since I know better, I'm going to fuck your ass while Tommy does his best to get in and out of your tight pussy. Maybe then you'll learn there's no escaping us."

Another stinging slap, another yelp.

This time, I swallow the vitriol I want to spew at Clay.

He can tell. Trading his spanks for a gentle caress, he calls out, "Tommy?"

"Yeah… yeah, Clay?"

Oh. Tommy's *close* close. No wonder he stopped moving. Considering he seemed to mastermind this whole thing, it's not performance anxiety or something like that that kept him from fucking me harder once Clay took my ass. Nope. He's about to go off like a rocket, but he's listening to Clay. Until they got to share me, he wouldn't come.

Now? All bets are off—and Clay knows that, too.

"Can you reach Cyn's clit?"

His hand shifts. Our bodies are slick with sweat, lube, and the juices from my pussy, but he manages to shove his fingers between us, finding my clit. My answering squeal as he rubs the super sensitive nub is all Clay needs to know, but Tommy still says, "She's so fucking hot, Clay. Her clit is huge, and I can see how we have her split open. This is the sexiest fucking thing I've ever seen. God, Cyn, you're *gorgeous*."

He lifts his head off the pillow, trying to kiss me. I want to refuse. I'm being fucked by two killers I thought I knew—I thought I *loved*—but for Tommy to kiss me while Clay is slowly rocking in my ass? If he hadn't pinched my clit, forcing my lips to part as I cried out in pleasure, I never would've let him in.

But I do, and no matter what Clay had seen while he stalked Tommy and me over the years, watching his best friend nip my bottom lip, shove his tongue in my mouth, and kiss me like he owns me… it makes my murderous husband even more dangerous.

Clay won't hurt me. As vulnerable as I am—and I don't just mean in this position—I know he won't. But he does increase the pressure as he pulls out just enough for the full sensation to subside a little before returning tenfold. I gasp again, and with his slippery hand, he grabs my hair, tugging my head back.

Now Clay's kissing me, and it never even occurs to me to deny him his kiss. And I know, as the possessive way Clay claims me—plus how my back bent to accommodate him—finally sets Tommy off enough that he's coming inside of me, that whatever happens when this night is over, Clay was right.

I can't deny him anything.

SANDWICHED BETWEEN THE ONLY TWO MEN I'VE EVER loved, I should feel like the luckiest fucking woman in the world.

Clay is spooning me, his body pressed against my back. Strangely enough, he's still half-naked. After our shower—where he refused to pull off his t-shirt, as though he's hiding something beneath it… like the slice I gave him earlier?—he swapped the soaked shirt out for his hooded sweatshirt while Tommy was taking his time, drying me off with a towel. Clay went without his jeans, though, leaving his cock nestled between my thighs. He's hard again, but he's also snoring softly as he clutches me to him.

Running around an island, killing all our old friends, then having his cock sucked, his side slashed, and nutting three times since he first told me to crawl to him? My poor psycho husband. He must be *exhausted*. He didn't even try to fuck me one last time after the two of them herded me to bed. Clay just pulled me up against him, promised me again that there's no getting away from my husband, then promptly went to sleep.

Despite my situation, I feel a familiar pang in my chest. That's Clay. Man could pass out anywhere, then wake up instantly without an alarm after the deepest, most restful sleep. That's *my* Clay... only my Clay is undeniably a ruthless killer who plotted with his best friend for the last five years to wear me down, get me to accept that I belong to both of them, then kill everyone I knew—everyone they believed ever wronged me—as a twisted way to make amends.

Some girls get flowers and diamonds. I get my former tormentors trussed up, mutilated, *tortured*, plus a side of double penetration as they both needed to fuck me at the same time just to really send home the message that they believed I was *theirs*.

It's hard to deny that. Clay is at my back. Tommy is sleeping in front of me, completely naked instead of half, and just as possessive. His hand is on my hip, the other one reaching out toward my hair, fingers twining around the damp clumps that haven't dried all the way yet.

Clay likes my hair long. Clay likes my hair down. After our shower, he handed Tommy the brush, watching in approval as my boyfriend untangled the hair that Clay shampooed and conditioned in the shower. When Tommy admitted he wasn't so sure how to pull my hair up the way I like after it's been washed, Clay took the brush away from him.

He likes it down. It's down.

Clay likes me to sleep naked. Like Tommy, I don't have a stitch on.

At least I'm clean. My body feels like it's been hit by a truck since it's definitely not used to being fucked like that, but Tommy pulled a pain reliever bottle out of his duffel bag. Clay dropped two in my mouth, then handed me a can of ginger ale to chase it down so that I wouldn't be as achy in the morning.

After all, it'll be Monday. If all goes well, we're leaving tomorrow.

Do they realize that there are five dead bodies on the island? Six if you count what happened to Aaron? I'm sure they do. Fuck, they planned this for *five years*. I'm sure they have something up their sleeves, just like I'm betting they think I'll be that timid heroine, that meek little girl who simply goes along with it.

Clay and Tommy are treating me like I am. As soon as they both finished, they were careful to take care of me. I guess that's the dominant nature that Clay's always had and that Tommy obviously suppressed. They fucked me like they didn't care if I broke, and when I didn't, the killer and his accomplice pampered me like I was precious. They used my body until I was a trembling, sweaty, sticky mess between them, and as I came down from being fucked by the both of them at the same time, Tommy stroked my hair out of my face. Clay peppered kisses down my back, telling me how good I was, how impressed he was that I took them both so well, and how it'll be that much easier next.

Next time…

I didn't argue. My mind whirring, both with the realization that they're serious, that this is happening, that my life is set... I let them do whatever the fuck they wanted to me because, well, I'm beginning to understand that that's what they expect from me.

By the time they learn that that's not true, I'm hoping to have a plan of my own.

Until then, I played my part as my husband disposed of the condom he pulled on to take my ass. While I laid on my side, honestly too spent to move, he stroked his semi-hard cock, gathering up as much of the come that clung to him after he pulled the condom off. Then, dipping his finger between my legs, he scooped up some of Tommy's load, swirling their jizz together, then went a step further than shooting come on my chest. He swiped it on my lips before fisting my hair, tilting my head back, kissing me so deeply, I was light-headed before he finally pulled back.

He did all of this while Tommy watched, his expression hungry, his cock already twitching again.

He wanted to fuck me. Since I took Tommy back, I learned that he could go as many times as I could take him. Once was never enough for him, and I always got the impression that he was making up for lost time.

Now I know better. Now I know that he was doing his best to catch up to the number of times *Clay* fucked me so that, by the time they agreed to share me, they'd be even—and I'd be so addicted to both of them, I'd go along with this madness.

He stroked himself, almost whimpering as Clay tasted

the combination of all three of us he forced onto my lips. But he didn't move. As much as he obviously wanted to stick his dick back inside of me, he waited to see what Clay wanted to do first.

And what Clay wanted to do was carry me bridal-style to the bathroom where the three of us had a very cramped shower in the shower stall. Once we were clean and I felt semi-human again, after I was dried off, he dressed me while Tommy changed the sheets on our bed so that, when he guided us to lay down in our spots, there was no mess to lie in.

Clay fell asleep first. Tommy murmured all of the things that he was looking forward to doing now that we were going to be a committed trio.

We'll have to leave Gullhaven, of course. The whole fucking world still thinks Clayton Rivers is dead, and with Clay funneling money into an LLC that Tommy had access to, it was better that they did. I half-listened to him, waiting for the post-nut clarity to fade to post-nut exhaustion. Tommy cuddled closer, falling asleep, while I refused to.

Their breathing is even. Both of the guys are *out* out. I'm still super careful as I unthread Tommy's fingers from my hair. It takes a few seconds to remove his hand from my hips, listening intently for any change in his breathing. When he doesn't react, I focus on disentangling myself from Clay's tight hold.

That takes longer, but I'm determined. Before, I was too stunned by the events of the night to fight back. I tried, even drew a little of Clay's blood, but he was right. If I wanted to kill him, I could've.

That's not what I want. Beyond that, I don't know…

I'm confused. Hurt. Feeling extremely betrayed. I'm also irrationally happy that my husband seemed to return from the dead, even if he came back just in time for Halloween as a Michael Myers-Jason wannabe.

I mean, I *could* kill them. As I slip off the bottom side of the bed, the two completely unaware that I'm almost gone, I know that both Tommy and Clay have their weapons in this cabin. Chase's gun is useless now, but anyone can kill if they put their minds to it. Having a large knife like Clay's or even a switchblade like Tommy's will make it so damn easy.

But I *don't* want to. So, instead, I pull on the first sleep shirt I can find, slip my feet into a pair of sneakers, grab my phone for the flashlight I could've used earlier, then disappear into the night.

WELCOME TO
HALO ISLAND
'til death
do we part...

NINETEEN

SACRIFICE

When I hear the telltale sounds of heavy footsteps crackling against the dried-up leaves in the forest, I glance at my phone.

It takes a good half an hour to reach Halo Lake if you're walking at a quick pace. Cut that in half if you're jogging. Based on how long I've been sitting at the water's edge, watching it shimmer in the moonlight, whoever is out there must've hauled ass the whole way here and only slowed his run to a speed walk as he approached the lake.

I can't tell from the steps who is out there, though I'm pretty sure it's only one man. Less than a minute later, when Clay pops his head out of the woods before stalking the rest of the way toward me, I give myself an imaginary pat on the back.

If I had to bet, I would've put money down that Clay would figure out I was here first.

And maybe that's why I came here to have this confrontation. Tommy said that we needed to take this trip to Halo Island to build new memories, to forget the bad ones that haunted me my entire life. Naively, I thought he was just talking about our weekend getaway. I know better now, that these two men expect my entire life to change after this most recent time on the island. One way or another, they're right.

"*Cyn*," he says, the relief in his voice obvious. "I've been looking everywhere for you. I woke up, and you were gone."

Huh. Hurts, doesn't it?

He firms his jaw when I don't react. "No, baby. I told you. We're all done with that shit. There's no more walking away. Not for any of us. You understand me?"

I still don't answer him. Instead, I trail my finger through the mud at the edge of the water, wordlessly inviting him closer.

He takes my continued silence as my agreement. That's fine. By the time morning rolls around in a handful of hours, one thing's for sure: my husband will know exactly *what* I understand about all of this—and what I think about it, too.

Clay's fully dressed again. From his black hooded sweatshirt to his black jeans, his black boots, and the knife sheathed at his waist… the only thing that's missing is the matte mask from before. I guess, now that the truth is out—and there's no one left on the island who could identify him—he doesn't need it.

My gaze flickers to the worn handle of his large knife. He shouldn't need that, either, but he brought it.

Interesting. Very, very interesting.

Clay sits down next to me, so close that our hips are touching. "You scared me, baby. I get it. Why you snuck away… I always knew where you were, even when I had to play dead. This was the first time I didn't. You scared me fucking shitless, Cyn. That's all. Don't do that."

Again, I stay quiet, staring at the water instead of the man who should be a ghost.

He clears his throat, too real to be a phantom. "You told me once that I didn't know what it was like to watch someone die." His gaze slides my way. "To take a life."

I did. It was in a fit of anger one time when Clay was treating me like I was so fragile, he was expecting me to shatter. I hated it then, and I loathe it now. I like to be pampered, sure, but also respected. That's why I'd often show my husband that I was never as weak as he obviously thought I was. It was only fair. If anyone knew what exactly I was made of, it should've been Clayton Rivers, but whenever he forgot, I reminded him.

Like I'm going to do now.

Still, he does manage to pull two words from me: "I know."

Clay fingers the handle of his knife. "I've killed four. Slaughtered most of them. So now I *do* know."

"You say that so easily," I whisper into the night.

"Because it *was* easy," he admits. "They hurt you."

That's what he keeps saying. That this insane plan my

two lovers—former and current and current *again*—came up with hedged on the idea that my former 'friends' terrorized me in their own way and, because of that, they needed to die for Tommy and Clay to prove how serious they were about the three of us banding together, us against the rest of the fucking world.

But doesn't he get it? Aaron and Tyler were sacrifices in the grand scheme of things, and if everything Clay told me was true, then Summer and Madison, Chase and Vee… they fucked up my high school years, hurting me in ways that still traumatized me a decade later.

Even so, the one person in this world who destroyed me the most? Is the man sitting next to me who doesn't seem to understand just what it did to me to lose him.

"*You* hurt me," I tell Clay.

"I did what I had to because I fucking adore you," Clay says, and I can't tell if he's pleading with me to believe him—or terrified I won't. "I would never hurt you on purpose."

Does that matter? On purpose or not, I never got over Clay. "I loved you."

"Loved? *Loved?* You still love me, Cyn. You have to."

Once again, I think: I don't have to do anything.

I gave in to my lust for my two lovers earlier because I wanted to. If only for one night… I let them win. I let them have me.

But this game we've been playing on the island?

It isn't over yet, and as I sat next to the edge of Halo Lake, waiting to see who would find me first… if either of them would've known to follow me here… I accepted I wouldn't give up until I *won* it.

And my 'dead' husband knows it.

Clay curses under his breath. "Don't you get it? Hurting you… that was the last thing I wanted to do. I knew you loved me then, Cyn, like you better love me now. If you didn't, I really would've chosen death over just pretending until I could find my way back to you. But you have to know… I've always accepted you could never love me as much as I've always loved you. It just isn't possible. You could live without me if you had to, but baby, I can *never* live without you."

That's another thing he told me back at the cabin, and I have as hard of a time coming to grips with that now as I did then.

I want so badly to believe Clay while, at the same time, resisting the very strong urge to smack him so hard, his brain rattles around inside of his skull.

How could my husband believe I didn't love him as much as I did—*do*? Okay. So Maybe I didn't when we first got together—I had no idea how obsessed he was with me at the beginning, or how he'd waited years for me to notice him while I dated Tommy—but once I fell for him that fateful summer, I fell *hard*.

I don't remind him that he managed to live without me for five years. I already did, and I'm not in the mood for him to tell me again how he purposely stalked me the whole time so that he didn't have to 'exist' without me. Does he care that he made me convinced I was fucking crazy? Seeing things that weren't there? Clinging to the hope that he was alive only to have him reappear like he did nothing wrong?

What does he want? Acceptance? Forgiveness?

No. I know the answer.

Clayton Rivers desires what he always has: my complete and total surrender.

Only one problem, babe. I'm not seventeen anymore, and if he thinks he can manipulate me… *blackmail* me… he has another think coming.

Instead, I grit my teeth. "Losing you fucking *broke* me, Clay. Do you understand that? I was *shattered*. My heart still has cracks in it."

"I know. Don't *you* get *that?*"

I scoff.

"I mean it," Clay insists. His voice is a rumble deep in his chest as he tells me, "That's why I needed this grand fucking gesture to work my way back into your life. I know you. I still do. I could say I was sorry with words. I could tell you I love you and pray you knew I meant it. But I chose to show you my devotion in blood, and my remorse with as many lives as I could end—and I did it all for you.

"Now I know what it's like to kill, and if I have to do it again, I'm ready. Nothing will keep us apart anymore, Cyn. Fucking *nothing.*"

We'll see about that.

I glance over at him, meeting the insanity in his gaze. "For me?" I ask, daring him to answer. "Come on. You sure you didn't just kill them because I'd forgiven them, and they were actually my friends now?" Life doesn't end in high school, right? We'd tolerated each other since my return to Gullhaven, and even if I'd fantasized about killing Summer Kaye, I wouldn't have *done* it… "That they all had to die because you're a possessive asshole who acts like he can share, but never learned how?"

I'm not exaggerating, either. I didn't mind it at the time, but when Clay and I were together, he didn't like the idea of me having any friends other than him. That led to his controlling side insisting that I don't work or leave the house if I didn't have to. He had this grand idea that our life should include only the two of us, and I was so obsessively in love with him in return, I didn't care.

That makes me wonder. Is that why it always seemed like I was an outsider when it came to Tommy's friend group? Because, deep down, I was better with one person… *my* person?

"I killed them because it was the only way I could think to prove to you my devotion," he says again. "You never thought I had the balls to do it."

"Clay—"

"No. It's okay. We both know it's true. I'd do anything for you. I know you wondered how far I'd go. Well, damn it, Cyn. I 'died' for you. I killed for you. And now, when you tell me what kind of nerve it takes to take a life, I can tell you I know all about that." He waits a beat, then says, "How about you, Cyn? Was it easy?"

I go still. "Was what easy?"

"When you killed your mom. I never asked. I figured you had your reason, and it worked out for me in the long run, so it didn't matter. But was it easy?"

I refuse to answer him, and I'll give Clay a shred of credit: he knows better than to push me on that.

Maybe I shouldn't have lured him to the lake. It's where my life changed forever, but if I want to think about the true beginning of our love story, I have to admit it begins with the night I drowned my mother.

He's right, though. We don't talk about that. After he threatened to out me as a murderer if I didn't do what he wanted, we came to a silent agreement. My mother drowned. It was an accident. It was suicide. It wasn't murder.

Clay and I were fucking? Oh, no. I fell for his charm and his generosity after he invited me—no, not forced, why would you say forced?—to move into his home after my mother died. I wasn't being blackmailed. I was a foolish girl in love who cheated on her loyal boyfriend because she couldn't resist his best friend, the star kicker on the football team.

You mean the boy so obsessed with me, he stalked me on the island, following me while I was completely unaware that he was there? The boy who watched as my mother thrashed and I kept her head under the water, only releasing her when she went still and floated away?

You mean Clay, the man whose own twisted nature was a perfect complement to mine before he disappeared and returned to me a fucking serial killer?

Because he's not done. I can sense the bloodlust emanating off of him as he drops his hand on my thigh possessively. If I try to leave him, he won't kill me. I believe that to the depths of my soul. He won't kill me, but anyone who stands between us is a goner.

Staring at the water, ignoring the way he's boring a hole in my head with his gaze, I smile.

"Look at me, Cyn."

No. I can't always give him what he wants. He doesn't expect me to, either. If I always obeyed him, it wouldn't make it special when I did something like crawling to him because I wanted his dick in my mouth so damn bad—

"I said fucking *look at me*."

My smile widens.

Ah. There's *my* Clay. I had begun to wonder if the five years messed him up as much as it has me. A killer I can handle. But a man who doesn't lose complete control the first time he thinks he doesn't have my complete attention?

That would never work.

"You're begging." I take my time, turning so that we're staring into each other's eyes. "What happened to the masked killer who kept a knife in reach while I sucked his dick? The one who had to mark me with come, then fucked my ass next to Chase Whitmore's dead body because he knew Tommy never has?"

Clay has the decency to look a little ashamed at his actions.

"I was riding high on a cocktail of pent-up sexual aggression, bloodlust, and jealousy, " he admits. "It's a dangerous combination. But *you* were never in any danger, Cyn. You are *my wife*."

I was. Am I still?

I guess we'll see.

With a sigh, I ask, "Clay… why did you come here?"

"Because I knew I'd find you at the lake. You have history." He cradles the back of my head, tugging me close so that our foreheads are touching. "*We* have history."

"That's not what I meant," I whisper.

"We told you why it had to be on Halo Island."

Because this was the beginning—and the end.

I jerk out of his hold. He lets me, though his stare has turned unblinking.

He still doesn't get it, does he?

"Why did you come back?" I ask, and when his expression hardens, I think he finally does. "Forget your stupid fucking plan. You disappeared, and I was finally—"

"Happy?" he supplies.

I shrug. If that's what he wants to call it.

In the distance, I swear I hear more footsteps. The way Clay's ears cock before he jumps to his feet, holding out his hand to help me up, tells me that he heard it, too.

Before we're interrupted, though, he runs his thumb along the height of my cheek. "You weren't happy, Cyn. You were content." His stroke becomes rougher, and I hate how he knows me so well. *Content…* that's what I thought, too. "You missed me. Pretend you didn't if you want to. I know better. You *need* me."

Maybe. Maybe not.

The footsteps are closer now. We wait. Clay drops his hand, hooking his thumb in his belt loop. My skin burns from where he touched me.

Jesus fucking Christ. What is taking Tommy so damn long?

I thought he'd be right behind Clay. If they're partners like they want me to believe, wouldn't Clay have grabbed Tommy by the shoulder, shaken him awake, then barked at him to get some damn pants on? He should've been seconds behind Clay, but it's been nearly ten minutes that we've been alone.

That tells me that Clay *didn't* want Tommy to follow.

And I cling to that as I get up and walk toward Tommy right as he bursts through the trees, eyes panicked and curls flat, all while Clay lets me walk past him, then falls into step behind me.

WELCOME TO
HALO ISLAND

'til death
do we part...

"**W**hat are you two doing?" Tommy asks, just winded enough that I know he ran the entire way here once he realized that this was where we'd be. "If you wanted to go for a swim, you should've told me. I would've come."

I get that now. It isn't that one of these men is more dominant than the other, or that one is the mastermind, the other the follower. Both of them want one thing. Both will do whatever they have to to get that one thing. Nothing will stop them.

Except, you know, maybe that *one thing* has an opinion of her own.

From the moment I let the both of them use me, I realized that—despite their claims to both be obsessively, *murderously* in love with me—I would always be the goddamn chew toy being tugged between them.

Like Clay, he took the time to get dressed. Like Clay, he knew to find me here.

Of course. Clay let the cat out of the bag on *that* one while he had me tucked between him and Tommy after they finished with me.

I guess it was obvious I was still stuck on Tommy having sex with Summer after we were together. And that's when Clay dropped one last bomb on me: I thought that he was the only one who knew that I drowned my mother in Halo Lake. He was the one who saw me do it, and who used it to get everything he wanted out of me.

But somehow, Summer knew. All her snide comments weren't simply alluding to my mother's suspicious death. She honestly was convinced I'd drowned her, and when she confronted Tommy with the truth after he started dating me again, threatening to tell the cops instead of just spreading rumors around Gullhaven, he asked her what it would take to earn her silence.

In her way, Summer was as selfish and manipulative as Clay because all she wanted was a lover who didn't belong to her.

And like I did, fucking Clay that first time, Tommy agreed to be with Summer on the side so long as she left the past in the past.

It wasn't the reality that Clay was alive and still friends with Tommy that they were covering up for every time Tommy left me to fuck Summer. It was how she was blackmailing him with some kind of proof that I murdered my own mom to get him to choose her over me in any way she could. Whenever he fell out of line, she got her kicks fucking with me, even bringing Madison in on it, and Tommy had to bide his time.

So he plotted her murder even as he plowed her, and to his last breath, he would forever be convinced he did it for me.

He didn't care that I snapped and showed I was capable of murder. Nope. He actually became a murderer himself for me, just like Clay, so he could *understand* me better.

I never knew he had found out the truth about that night on Halo Island; probably from Clay, but when I asked, he kissed that spot behind my ear that had me so distracted, I forgot what we were talking about. Over the years, Tommy's never made it clear he had any idea. I guess, following Clay's lead in that, too, he refused to bring it up because I've spent the last ten years deluding myself into believing that my mother's death was an unfortunate accident, not the result of a narcissistic, impulsive teenage girl feeling the sting of rejection for the first time.

But I've never been able to take being rejected well, and when my mother did it… I can't say I had *meant* to hurt her, but it happened, and she only had herself to blame.

On that fateful weekend in May, my mother made it very clear that, now that I was almost eighteen, I was no longer the most important person in her life. She was choosing Rick over me. She was *rejecting* me.

She had to die.

Seventeen-year-old Cyn thought that was a fairly simple assessment. My mom didn't love me. My mom didn't deserve to live.

And I killed her.

It wasn't premeditated. Everything else that led up to her actual death was true. My mom didn't return to the cabin, but that was because she was walking by the lake, trying to find the words to tell me that she was moving Rick into our house after graduation, and that she expected me to move out and start a life of my own.

I wasn't even eighteen and she wanted me gone.

Is it any wonder that I snapped and pushed her into the lake? That when she struggled to get up, yelling at me for getting her wet, I just wanted her fucking mouth to shut up?

She couldn't yell at me under the water. And once she was dead, she couldn't love Rick anymore. She couldn't choose him over me.

What if these two decide to choose each other? They haven't yet. They both want me to choose them… but what if that changes? For seventeen years, my mom chose me until she didn't.

I've already lost five years with one man, then five with the other. I was a widow at twenty-two. I'm twenty-seven now. I don't want to start over again.

"We're not swimming, Tommy," I say needlessly,

considering Clay and I have moved away from the lake, joining him near the edge of the trees. "But we're having a long overdue chat."

"Oh. Okay. Well, I don't want to miss that."

No. He really doesn't.

"You both know a lot about me, huh? You'd have to to predict my reactions over the years… to manipulate me into getting what you both want. Well, I think there's something you forgot during all of that. Know what it is?"

Clay's watching Tommy out of the corner of his eye. His hand hasn't left the handle of his knife.

In his hand, Tommy's holding his folded switchblade. Interesting. Maybe they *do* know everything about me…

Just in case, I give them a little hint. "I'm an only child," I tell them. "You now what *that* means?" I wait a beat, then shrug. "I don't share."

"Cyn—"

"You love me," I say to Tommy.

"I would've waited forever for you," he swears. "Five years. Ten. However long it took for you to give me a second chance, I would've waited."

I know.

Turning to Clay, I remind him, "You said you can't exist without me."

Clay sets his jaw. His formerly boyish features turn sharp, a deadly edge to the man I mourned for five years. He's older now, but that danger that was always there, even as a teenager… whether it's the memory I have of the blood splattered all over his face from earlier tonight or the handle of the knife sticking out of the sheath he pulled back on before he left the cabin, he's absolutely *murderous.*

His voice drops. "You are my wife. You are my everything."

If I was his everything, he wouldn't have left me. If Tommy cared that much about me, he wouldn't have fucked Summer to earn her silence once we were together. He'd have killed her, made it seem like an accident, made her go away.

One man left me.

One man cheated.

I'm a hypocritical bitch. I cheated first, and even when a part of me inexplicably sensed that Clay couldn't be dead, that he *had* to be alive, I allowed myself to walk away from my vows, starting up a new life with Tommy.

And it infuriates me that it wasn't my choice. Not really.

They took the choice away from me. If I knew my options, would there ever have *been* a choice?

I know the answer to that. And now it's time I'm going to make *them* choose.

One night. I let them have their one night. But if these men loved me as much as they claim, if I'm their obsession—their possession—like they think… they should've known me better.

They should've known that I need to be number one.

Tommy Gillis and Clayton Rivers are best friends.

They planned this, *plotted* it, and executed it. Not only that, but they executed the mean girls, the bullies from my past, the asshole who sexually assaulted me in high school. Anyone who knows what happened to Caroline Preston is worm food now, and I'm facing off against the two men I've ever loved. Two men who were so desperate to have me, they concocted this scheme to manipulate me, to gaslight me, to put me through hell itself just so they could both claim me in the end.

But I don't share—and it's time they understood that.

I smile, tucking a lock of my still-damp hair behind my ear. "Yeah? Then prove it."

Tommy's expression turns puzzled. "Cyn? What are you saying?"

"You love me. But you love each other, too."

That's undeniable. Only a deep bond like the one that Clayton Rivers and Tommy Gillis have would've allowed them to spend ten fucking years on a plan that ended with both of them having the one thing they wanted: *me*. Screw their plan. Why do they get what they want?

What about me?

"I want that love," I tell them simply. "I deserve it. And the loyalty… you killed for me. Protected my secrets. But that's not enough."

It's never been enough. Not for someone like me. Broken. Twisted. Selfish.

Demanding.

"One of you has to love me most of all," I purr.

"More than yourself. More than your best friend." Now I shrug, dropping my hands to my waist, fisting my hips as I dare them both: "Prove it."

Clay understands what I'm saying first. His cheeks hollow as he sucks in a breath, but he doesn't say a word. Not to Tommy. Not to me. Instead, he twitches his fingers, then unsheathes his knife.

And then it happens, and my girlish heart fucking squeals.

My husband spins on his heel, slashing out with the blade. It drags across his best friend's throat, leaving an open gash in its wake.

"Sorry, Tommy," Clay utters, voice entirely flat as the blood starts to spill. "But I was an only child, too."

It takes Tommy a second to notice what happened. That's how quick Clay struck. No wonder he was able to take down each of the island's guests one by one without any trouble. With reflexes honed from years of athletics and instincts that belong to a born killer, he not only sliced without hesitation. He did it so effortlessly, Tommy's only reaction is to reach for his throat while stumbling toward me.

"Would've waited…" He gasps, blood bubbling in the corner of his mouth as he drops to his knees, still clutching his throat. "*Forever.*"

This is because of me. Looking away from the absolute proof of Clayton's jealousy and possessiveness… I won't do that. Just like how I didn't even blink until my mother stopped thrashing under the water, I'll witness Tommy's death, too.

I step toward him at the same time as Clay steps back, allowing me to approach the dying man, and stroke his jaw when I'm near enough to touch him. "I know, Tommy. But you never got it, did you? I made my promise. I made my vow. It's 'til death do we part for Clay and me, and not even him being dead could make me stop loving him. You would've waited forever—"

He's gurgling. *Choking.* Once I take my hand back, he jerks, like he's trying to keep the connection, but I'm already at Clay's side. I lay my hand on his elbow right as Tommy falls forward, then flops onto his back, twitching as he dies.

I *tsk*, only a tiny bit remorseful.

"—but I already promised it to someone else."

<hr>

AND THEN THERE WERE TWO.

Tommy is dead. Unlike the other murders, Clay made it quick so that he wouldn't suffer… much. Even so, my former lover turned his head, watching me with adoration in his dark blue eyes until the moment life winked out of them.

I didn't turn away from him. Unlike Chase, I owed Tommy that much.

He loved me. Tommy Gillis loved me enough to wait.

To be a shoulder to cry on, and the man who accepted that he would always be second place in my heart. He loved me enough to take whatever scraps I tossed his way, even knowing that I would always be Clayton Rivers' wife.

He loved me—just not more than Clay did.

His eyes were wide open and still staring after he gasped his last breath. Clay bent low to close Tommy's lids, then clicked his tongue when he saw that Tommy never even had the chance to flip open his switchblade before Clay sliced his throat.

Rising up, he looks at the blood on his knife. A few quick swipes against his dark jeans, and the blade is clean again.

He clears his throat, and when he speaks, I can't tell if it's bloodlust from his recent kill or actual lust for his wife that has his voice so damn husky. "So, am I forgiven yet, baby?"

I don't pretend not to know what he's asking me. But, instead of answering him, I say, "Five lives. Aaron. Vee. Tyler. Summer. Tommy. One for every year you made me live without you. Think that's enough?"

Something about my voice makes it clear to both of us that *I* don't.

His head shoots over to meet my gaze. "I'd give you the whole fucking world if that's what you want. Slaughter them all and lay their heads at your feet, Cyn. I worship you. I always have. Last night was just the start. I'll do anything for you."

My lips curve. Clay… he's always known the right things to say to catch my attention.

He worships me?

Good.

I point to the grass. "Then get on your knees."

After all, it's his turn.

He doesn't even bother sheathing his knife. Tossing it to the side, he goes to the ground, watching me closely, waiting to see what I'm going to do.

I can't help myself. The first time I ever slept with Clay, I did it along this very lake. It was his idea, but I won't pretend that I was forced into it. Blackmailed, sure. Manipulated, definitely. But though I was loyal to Tommy until my mother told me she was remarrying and I *snapped*, when Clay stepped out of the trees and said, "I saw what you did," and I offered him whatever he wanted to keep quiet, I never in a million years thought he'd want *me*.

It started out as sex. I refused to dump Tommy when I wasn't even sure that Clay wouldn't get what he wanted, then turn me in when he got bored. But that was when I was too oblivious to realize that my boyfriend's best friend had been secretly obsessed with me since freshman year. By the time we were seniors at GHS, he was sure he'd never get his chance—until he took it.

In a way, we were like Summer and Tommy, weren't we? I gave Clay my body for his silence. Even before I went to live at the Rivers house—just another way he manipulated me, getting me close and tearing me away from Tommy—I knew what I was doing was wrong. I was cheating on Tommy, fucking his best friend behind his back.

But it was only sex then. I had no intention of falling for Clay, and since I didn't plan on killing again, I had to do what I had to do to keep him quiet.

Then he demanded more from me. He demanded *all* of me. I ended things with Tommy when I admitted that I wanted Clay for myself, and knowing that I was the only one Clay loved… but he left me, and I'm not sure if I can ever get over that.

So I made him kill Tommy. Why not? It's only fair he's the one to make sacrifices this time.

Still. My blood is undeniably pumping. He chose *me*, didn't he? Without a second thought, this new incarnation of Clay slaughtered his oldest friend, and he did it for *me*. He loves me, and the thrill of being so fucking essential to him that he'd discard a decade-long plan because I demanded it…

I fucked Clay after I killed my mom. Now I'm going to fuck him after he killed Tommy.

And my 'dead' husband isn't going to stop me.

WELCOME TO
HALO ISLAND

'til death
do we part...

TWENTY-ONE
FOR YOU

He's on his knees. Folding my sleep shirt under mine, I lower myself until I'm in front of him. My fingers dance across the bulge behind his jeans; like me, it looks like a little murder turns him on, too, but I already knew that.

Flicking open his button, tugging down the zipper easily… his hard cock all but jumps into my waiting palm.

I close my fingers around him and tug.

His eyes flutter closed. *"Cyn…"*

"You crept into my bed. You fucked me and never let me know you were there. You got me on my knees…" I twist the head of his cock, enjoying the control I have over this killer as his eyes snap back open. "You made me crawl, Clay."

He smirks. "You loved it, baby. Admit it."

Of course I did. Even when I was sure *he* snapped

and wasn't the man I married, when Clayton Rivers says crawl, I listen.

But I refuse to admit it. Not until he makes the last five years up to me… "No."

"You love me. I know you do. Tell me, Cyn. Tell me I'm still your husband."

Is that a hint of panic I hear? He deserves it. "'Til death do we part," I remind him for a second time. "That's what we promised, right? Everyone thinks you're dead."

"Then I'll marry you again," snarls Clay, his hand going to my throat. He collars it, tugging my head down so that our mouths are inches apart. "You and me, we go on that ferry. We get the fuck out of Gullhaven. We start over… I'll give you the wedding of your dreams, leave this island behind. But you *are* my wife. Not even Tommy could've changed that."

I shiver, jerking out of his hold. "What would the next five years have looked like? The three of us together?"

"If it's the only way I could have you," he swears.

I actually believe that. Or, rather, that *Clay* believes he means it when he says that.

But he knows me. Even as a ruthless, blackmailing seventeen-year-old, Clay knew how I operated. So when I scoff and say, "Prove it," he doesn't just use his words.

Clay moves back just enough that he can reach down, grab the hem of his black sweatshirt, and rip it over his head. He tosses it, letting me see his bare chest for the first time since he returned to me.

At first, I thought he was pointing out the shallow slice cut into his side. But then he gestures higher, gruffly saying, "How's this for proof, baby," and I see exactly what he was hiding.

Clay's always been a man of action. In the securities world, even back in high school when it came to kicking the winning field goal for the championship, he *acts*.

And long before he started murdering in my name, when I thought he was dead and gone and buried an empty casket beneath a headstone with his name on it, he did *this*.

Clay was never as bulky as Tyler. Like Tommy, he was lean yet muscular, and the years apart only added definition to his hairless chest. He's cut, absolutely delicious, but though I appreciate the sight of his chest, it's what's on the left side of it that catches my attention now —and my breath.

Huh. No wonder he hadn't removed his shirt yet. If he wanted to prove some kind of point I'm still not sure I understand by double-teaming me with Tommy, he had to hide it. Because once I saw what he'd done…

Multiple puckered pink scars stand out over the white skin. Three letters had been carved over his nipple, each one about an inch-and-a-half high: **CYN**.

But that's not all. Beneath his nipple, curved over the bottom of his left pec, are four jagged slash lines in a row. They're of a similar size, similar length, but the scars look just unique enough to show they were cut at different times.

My lips part, fingers lifting to probe at the bottommost one as I see the evidence of my possession of this man. "Did you… did you carve my name into your chest?"

Because it totally looks like he *carved* my *name* into his *chest*.

He juts his chin out in pride, enjoying my stunned reaction. "See, baby? I practiced a little before I turned my knife on all those assholes. You could say I was my first canvas. Like it? I did it for you."

My throat feels thick. I swallow roughly. "It all looks so… old."

"It is. Most of it was done five years ago."

Oh.

Oh.

"Know what? That actually reminds me."

Clay rises up from his knees, crouching so he can search for the knife he abandoned. I don't even know that's what he's doing until he lashes out his hand, grabbing it, but before I can even react—or get the chance to wonder if I was wrong, if he *will* kill me—he's on his knees again, the point digging into the muscle of his chest.

He draws in a quick breath, then drags the knife over his skin, left to right. Not once does he look away from me as he does it, and when he lifts the knife, I see exactly what those four lines are now that a fifth has crossed them.

Tally marks.

"Clay? What did you do?"

I don't know why I ask that. It's pretty fucking obvious.

It's well past midnight now on October 28th. Five years ago, he disappeared. This is the fifth anniversary of what I thought was his death, but to Clay, it was the end of a self-imposed banishment.

And he has the marks on his chest to prove it.

"I never took off my ring," he vows, "so everyone who managed to see me knew I was married. That wasn't many, though. For five years, I was a ghost. I made money for our future. I planned for when I could come back. I stalked you because, damn it, Cyn, I was an addict, and just seeing your smile was the fix I needed. But in case anyone wondered who had my heart, I just echoed what it looks like on the inside. It's yours. It's always been yours."

"Five years," I whisper. "Why five?"

"Because he had you for four, and I wanted at least one year more than that," he whispers back. "He agreed to five if he got the next five. I wasn't thinking that far ahead. I… it was only about the next second I could call you mine."

If that's the case, then why would he ever give me up? If I meant that much to him?

I don't ask him. I don't *have* to.

"I made the deal with Tommy the day he confronted me about stealing you from him," Clay confesses, shaky and resigned and *frustrated* as he tosses the knife to the grass. He bats his cock with his free hand, but as though he knows better than to stroke himself while he's prostrate on his knees before me, he ignores his own need… for the moment. "Seventeen-year-olds think with their dick, and they're easily influenced. I never thought you'd stick around for more than that summer. Hell, you could've killed me and washed your hands off the whole thing. No one saw what happened but me. I thought I was the only witness. But you didn't, and I was terrified you would if Tommy came clean about the whole thing. So I did it. I let him blackmail me, and now…"

Clay's eyes dart toward Tommy's corpse. Once again, it looks like the two of us are sexually insatiable, ready to fuck next to a dead body. We should've known we'd never have a traditional relationship when he fucked me awkwardly, enthusiastically, *desperately* while my mother drifted on the surface of Halo Lake a decade ago.

And now…

He traces the scar on his chest with his fingertips, ghosting over them, smearing the blood welling up along the slice.

"You are my wife," he says again, with more meaning than even before. "From the moment I looked into your pretty brown eyes and I creamed my pants the first time, I knew it would be you. You just didn't know it yet. And that was okay. I scared myself with how much you went from being Cyndi, the quiet girl with her head down in middle school, to Cyn, the temptress I'd do anything to have.

"You chose Tommy then. He convinced me you'd do it again. Fuck it, Cyn. I just wanted you to be happy. I waited four years to call you mine for five. I waited five years for forever. I'm patient, baby," he adds, scooting toward me on his knees, cock jutting out of his groin, as Clayton fucking Rivers *crawls*. "But my patience is wearing thin. Please, *Mrs. Rivers*. Take mercy on your husband like you did to that Whitmore prick. I need you more than Tommy ever did, I fucking swear it."

"He's dead now." Leaning toward Clay, I run my thumb over the slit in his cock, gathering the precome. Giving him my own wicked grin, I dapple it with my tongue, then pinch his chin with my damp digit. "You regret that?"

"There is nothing I regret when it comes to you," he rasps. "Except for leaving. And I want you to understand, I will never, *ever* do that again."

My lips curve upward.

Good answer.

Hooking my leg around his hip, I angle his cock so that it's lodged at the entrance of my pussy, then sink down on him. Once I'm seated on his lap, I wrap my arms around his neck.

He wants mercy, and I gave him that by taking his cock inside of me. But if he expected forgiveness just because I climbed on his lap?

My husband needs to work a little harder than that.

"And what if I don't consider myself your wife anymore?" I ask him.

Clay's response is just as instant as when he tore off his shirt. He tilts his head back, breaking free of my loose embrace as he purposely bares his throat.

"Then kill me," he whispers, the sound ragged and almost daring. "Grab my knife. It's right there by your hand. Carve my heart out of my goddamn chest. At least if I die now, I'll die fucking the only woman I've ever loved."

And that does it. At that moment, I accept that this… all of this… was meant to be. Like Jack and Sally, me and Clay were meant to be.

But if he does try to pull some shit like this again—

My elbows rest on his shoulders, my fingers curving his cheeks. "Kill you? Why would I kill you? I just got you back, Clayton. But if you ever try to leave me again…"

He leans into my touch. "I never should've let Tommy convince me I had to. I was young. Stupid." His hands move to the small of my back, clutching me to him. "Fuck, Cyn, I was *guilty*. He was my best friend. My goddamn brother. And what did I do? I obsessed over his girl." He squeezes me through my shirt, bucking up as he bottoms out inside of me, forcing me to take everything he has to offer. "When I found a way to make you mine, I took it. You cheated on him with me because I made you, and I stole you away because I *needed* to—"

"You stole me because I wanted to be stolen." Still

caressing his skin, I trail my fingers down his blood-spattered face, stroking his jaw, then settling my hands around his neck again. As I rock on him, squeezing his cock, I dig my thumbs into his throat—and Clay groans. I smile. "You wanted me more. That's what counted. I wanted to be the most important person to someone. Tommy had his family. His friends. *Summer*," I spit out, using my nails to jab into his skin.

Clay quickens his thrusts, pounding up into my pussy as I draw blood. "Fuck, yes, Cyn. Do that *again*."

No. I pull out my nails, even as I'm careful not to lose the connection of his dick inside of me, before patting the crescent-shaped marks I left behind. "You chose him over me."

"Never—"

I stop moving. "Liar. Five years, Clayton. You abandoned me for *five fucking years*. Because you promised Tommy he could have a chance. But what about your promise to me?"

"I told you. I did it for you."

"Prove it," I repeat.

I taunted Clay with that earlier, and he killed Tommy. I did it again, and he showed me the scar on his chest.

What will he do now?

Clay drops his head to my neck, suckling my skin. He shifts his hips enough to make me fall forward on his lap, reminding me that I'm stuffed full of him. His teeth graze the side of my throat. I wanted to hurt him. Unless I'm imagining it, my murderous husband is trying to mark me with a hickey like we're seventeen again.

Angling my head, giving him better access to my neck, I let him.

He laps at my skin, the heat of his tongue sending shivers through me. My pussy contracts on his length, Clay sucking in a breath as I squeeze him.

"You loved him," he grates out at last. "When we were kids, you chose him first. Would you have picked me if I didn't force you to? If I didn't blackmail you into giving me all you could until I earned your heart?"

Would I have? I don't know, but it doesn't matter. From the moment Clay stepped out of the shadows, making it clear he watched me drown my mother, I had no choice. There was only one thing Clay wanted for his silence: *me*. First, in his house. Later, in his bed. He threatened to tell the truth about what happened on Halo Island if I didn't follow him to New Jersey, and by the time he asked me to be his wife—and I saw just how far he would go to make me love him—I never wanted to be separated from this man.

But Clay and Tommy had other plans, didn't they?

"I married you once," I remind him.

"Yeah, Cyn. And I told Tommy the trade was off once you had my ring on your finger." Lifting his head, Clay dips his chin so that he can find my hand. It's on his shoulder, and he reaches up, grabbing my left one with his right. "You are my wife. I couldn't share—"

I shake his hand off, then plant mine against his

chest. My right hand is still on his shoulder. Using Clay's body as leverage, I start to fuck him. Not just ride him. Not just sit on his lap, keeping his cock warm out in the late October breeze. The lake's chill has my arms covered in goosebumps, while the heat of Clay's strong body is all I need to stay hot, and after I purposely start bouncing on top of him, moving so quickly that he can barely match my rhythm, sweat starts beading up along my brow.

Clay wasn't expecting that. But if he thought that I'd forgiven him already, then he's forgotten exactly who his wife *is*. I'm not trying to get off myself, but as soon as he lays me out on the damp grass, switching our positions so that he's the one chasing his own nut, I slap him across the face with all the strength I can muster.

Did I need any further proof that the last five years apart changed my husband? Not really, but I get it in the way he reacts to me hitting him. Bracing his hands on both sides of my upper arms, caging me in, he comes with a roar, my name echoing across an island where only the dead can hear him.

Once Clay empties himself inside of me, he clutches my jaw, using his fingers to work my mouth open. And it is work. I'm not going to make it easy for him, not when my emotions are still a twisted mess, but as soon as he forces my lips apart, he slips his tongue into my mouth. It's a possessive kiss. A *claiming* kiss. The taste of him is so familiar, and the hint of metallic rust flooding my mouth after I purposely bit the edge of his tongue has me just about coming myself.

And that makes me *furious*.

Clay deepens the kiss after I bite him, but as soon as I stop kissing him back, he pulls away. His brow is furrowed, and for the first time since he removed the black plastic mask, I really feel like I'm looking at my husband again.

He's leaning on one elbow. One leg is thrown over mine, keeping me partly under him as his spent cock slips out of me.

"Baby?"

I spent years wishing I could be his 'baby' again. And now…

I grit my teeth. "I don't get it. If your stupid fucking deal was off, then what the hell was the last five years, Clay? You faked your death. You made me believe you were *gone*. That I'd never see you again. Because you chose Tommy, not *me*."

Lightning flashes across his face. "I told you, Cyn. *Never*."

I wish I could believe *that*—but when the evidence is right in front of me, I can't.

I shove him away from me.

Clay rolls onto his back; he obviously hadn't expected my push, or he would've held firm, keeping me pinned beneath him. Once he realizes that I'm starting to climb up, moving away from him, he shoots out his hand, lashing me around my wrist.

I don't resist. As he tugs me so that I'm sitting across his lap now, I let him get away with that, too.

"The deal was off. Listen to me… I called him. Said I was sorry, but I couldn't do it. Shit, Cyn… I was already losing my fucking mind, and I hadn't even left yet. I thought… there were times I thought I should just kill Tommy then and there so I could keep you for myself. He kept saying it was only five years, right? I got five to make you love me. He gets five to win you back. Then I reappear, and we both get to have you. But I was like, *fuck that—*"

Know what? I can honestly see two horny teenagers coming up with this insane idea. It was so simple, right? If I love them both, won't I be happy to call them both mine? But I was already so head over heels for Clay by the time we were married, he had to have known that I could never love anyone more than my husband.

"What changed?"

The muscle in Clay's cheek tics. "You were nice to him. When we went back to Gullhaven after my parents died. You were so happy to see him."

We've got to stop meeting at funerals…

I blink, some of my fury banking a little at that. "Clay. Seriously? He was there to pay his respects to your mom and dad. It was the first time I saw him after I left Gullhaven. It was awkward as fuck, babe, but I was nice to Tommy—for you."

He fists his hand, almost as though reaching for the knife he left on the ground somewhere. "I convinced myself he was right. It was only fair. I had my turn. Now he got his… but that meant I had to die. Even for you, Cyn, I couldn't fake wanting a divorce. To give you your chance with Tommy, I had to fake my death instead.

"What was five years compared to forever? You'd love us both… but it broke me, baby. Watching you live your life without me. Standing outside the window, watching you fuck Tommy… I shouldn't have blamed you before. If our plan worked, you were *supposed* to. But I was willing to share you with Tommy if I had to. No one else."

I use my thumb to rub off a few of the stray droplets of blood from Tommy's arterial spray. "There's no one left, Clay. You killed them all." Slipping the thumb between my lips, I swipe the dried blood with my tongue. I smile around the digit just like I did when I tasted his precome. "You're right. You did it all for me."

"Like I said. I'll do anything for you." He holds me tight, clutching me to him. Even if I wanted to get away, I couldn't. "Come on, Cyn. I fucked up. I fucked up bad. I think I've lost my mind, and I only found it when you fucked me just now. It's you and me. It's always been you and me. So… forgive me?"

Can I? "Not yet."

A ragged breath escapes Clay. "Cyn—"

"Not saying I won't. Five lives for five years without you… that's a good start. Proving how much you love me… that's a better one."

"I just wanted to give you everything you deserved," he tells me.

I have my husband back. The mean girls who made my time in high school a living hell? Gone. Anyone who might've known my secret? Dead men tell no tales, right? And Chase… the vindictive, remorseless part of me I've kept hidden these last ten years can't help but snicker to think that I got to swing the knife.

Mercy? Fuck that.

I got revenge—and Clay gave it to me.

He *loves* me.

"All I want is you."

We're trapped on an island with ghosts. Tomorrow morning, Mulligan is coming with the ferry. He's expecting two guests to leave—sorry, Tommy—and I'll be packed and ready to go with Clay. After that… I don't know what'll happen. That's something my mastermind of a murderous husband will have to figure out. After all, he and Tommy planned this. Tommy arranged for every single one of our 'friends' to come on this island, knowing he was sending them to their graves.

Clay actually used a fictitious LLC to *buy* Halo Island and set it up so that it would be the perfect trap for all of us.

But now that they've done what they set out to do, what was their plan when Clay's murder spree was done, and it was the three of us left standing? I'm not sure, but as I lean back, tilting my head invitingly as I part my lips for my husband's kiss, I don't care.

I have him back—and that's all I'll ever want.

WELCOME TO
HALO ISLAND
'til death
do we part...

NOVEMBER 2ND

THE GULLHAVEN GAZETTE

November 2   @gullhavengazette

MASSACRE ON HALO ISLAND:
IN A TRAGIC SCENE STRAIGHT OUT OF A HALLOWEEN HORROR FILM, MAN BRUTALLY MURDERS FIVE GUESTS, THEN HIMSELF.

Thomas Gillis (Instagram @carinhartbooks)

Six people are dead after a Halloween away on nearby Halo Island. When the ferry proprietor, Samuel Mulligan, returned on November 1st to retrieve the six guests and carry them back to Cottonwood Harbor, he walked into a scene that you'd find in any horror film: five young and promising Gullhaven locals had been murdered, seemingly by the sixth: Thomas Gillis, 28, a...

IN THE NOVEMBER 2ND EDITION OF THE GULLHAVEN GAZETTE:

MASSACRE ON HALO ISLAND: IN A TRAGIC SCENE STRAIGHT OUT OF A HALLOWEEN HORROR FILM, MAN BRUTALLY MURDERS FIVE GUESTS, THEN HIMSELF.

Six people are dead after a Halloween away on nearby Halo Island. When the ferry proprietor, Samuel Mulligan, returned on November 1st to retrieve the six guests and carry them back to Cottonwood Harbor, he walked into a scene that you'd find in any horror film: five young and promising Gullhaven locals had been murdered, seemingly by the sixth: Thomas Gillis, 28, also a lifelong resident.

An investigation is ongoing, but the confirmed victims are: Tyler Kaye, 29; Summer Kaye, 28; Madison Powell, 27; Violet Lee, 29; and Chase Whitmore, 28. Further information on services for the victims, as well as a vigil near City Hall, will be printed in a future edition of the Gazette.

Two other guests were also part of the excursion, though Mr. Mulligan confirms that he ferried them off of Halo Island four days before he returned for the victims. Nothing was amiss at the time, though Detective Jordan of the Gullhaven Police Department requests that, if you have any information on how to reach Cynthia Preston and Aaron Mueller for further questioning about this tragedy, please contact him at (555) 754-1003, extension 6.

WELCOME TO
HALO ISLAND
'til death
do we part...

NOVEMBER 20TH

THE GULLHAVEN GAZETTE

November 20   @gullhavengazette

MISSING LOCAL WOMAN DEAD:
CYNTHIA PRESTON. SURVIVOR OF THE HALO ISLAND HALLOWEEN MASSACRE, IS FOUND DEAD IN A CAR FIRE IN NEW YORK.

Cynthia Preston (instagram @carinhartbooks)

A Gullhaven woman who managed to escape the Halo Island massacre perpetrated by Thomas Gillis, then seemed to have vanished when the Gullhaven Police Department invited her in for questioning about the tragic event, has died. Cynthia Preston, 27, was involved in a car crash in Upstate New York, and perished when the vehicle she was in was engulfed in flames. When the police...

IN THE NOVEMBER 20TH EDITION OF THE GULLHAVEN GAZETTE:

MISSING LOCAL WOMAN DEAD: CYNTHIA PRESTON. SURVIVOR OF THE HALO ISLAND HALLOWEEN MASSACRE, IS FOUND DEAD IN A CAR FIRE IN NEW YORK.

A Gullhaven woman who managed to escape the Halo Island massacre perpetrated by Thomas Gillis, then seemed to have vanished when the Gullhaven Police Department invited her in for questioning about the tragic event, has died.

Cynthia Preston, 27, was involved in a car crash in Upstate New York, and perished when the vehicle she was in was engulfed in flames. When the police were called to the scene, the body was so damaged in the fire, dental records were needed to identify her. This led to Dr. Trent Vargas contacting Detective Jordan of the Gullhaven Police Department about her possible death.

At this time, it is confirmed that Ms. Preston was the sole passenger and casualty, and that this was an accident that has no correlation to the Halo Island Massacre. Ms. Preston is predeceased by her father, Steven Preston, her mother, Caroline Preston (who also tragically drowned on Halo Island a decade earlier), as well as her husband, Clayton Rivers, another Gullhaven local.

(*Editor's note:* Referring back to the edition printed on November 2, the Gullhaven Police Department were interested in making contact with Cynthia Preston and Aaron Mueller to discuss the tragic events that occurred on Halo Island. With the report of Cynthia's subsequent accidental death, Detective Jordan is still eager to speak with Aaron Mueller at (555) 754-1003, extension 6.)

WELCOME TO
HALO ISLAND

'til death
do we part...

EPILOGUE

There's something almost *amusing* when it comes to reading about your own death.

The article isn't an obituary, not really. I guess, if I want one of those, I'll have to invent some fictitious family member to submit it to the paper. I honestly didn't expect to see any news about my 'death' at all, though I did learn something from Tommy. After Clay and I staged the scene with the dead body and my smashed-up car, I set an online alert for my name to see what popped.

I did the same for Marla Hopps, the unfortunate blonde who was close enough to my age, my height, and my size to pass for my corpse. Clay only had her on ice for a few days while we did a little dental work and plotted how we would keep Detective Jordan off my ass, but it seems like we picked well. Doesn't look like anyone misses Marla since I haven't seen anything ping for her, but about two minutes ago, I got this notification.

The Gullhaven Gazette. I'm not surprised it's that online rag that picked up the story. The rest of the world didn't care about what happened on Halo Island—not ten years ago, not three weeks ago—but the hometown I could never truly escape… they just won't let its ghosts rest.

I know the only reason I made the main page on their site is because everyone in Gullhaven knows I was on the island before all the murders. That I immediately left made them curious. Clay and I both decided I needed to disappear before they became suspicious.

At this time, it is confirmed that Ms. Preston was the sole passenger and casualty, and that this was an accident that has no correlation to the Halo Island Massacre…

I shouldn't have doubted him. When he suggested I take a page out of his book and fake my own death, I didn't think it would work. But since our reunion on the island, we've been making a fresh start of things. He doesn't hold my time with Tommy over my head, and I try not to be bitter that I lost five years with my husband because of a stupid promise he made when he was a teenager.

Tommy is dead. Clayton Rivers, too. And, now, so is Cynthia Preston.

Is it too soon to move on? Maybe. I struggled to start over after I thought Clay was gone the first time, but now that I have him back and—as Mr. and Mrs. Clay Barker, newly 'married' and currently on their honeymoon on a tropical island far from California—I can't think of a better way to begin my second—*third*—chance at a happily-ever-after.

I have a husband who will do anything for me. I used to think Clay was the one with the upper hand, especially after the way he manipulated me into our relationship all those years ago, but after the island… I can't deny what I've always known.

I own this man. He 'died' for me. He *killed* for me. There isn't anything he won't give me, and now that Clay's seen just how fun the dark side can be, there's no going back. Not for either of us.

To take his place on the island, poor Aaron might have been Clay's first victim. He had never killed before he and Tommy set their convoluted plan into motion; not because of any morals he might have, but because it had never interested him before. He wanted me. *Just* me. And if he had to sacrifice all those lives, slaughter my friends —my tormentors—as penance for leaving me for Tommy to take, he would do it. He got a taste for it, though. The blood. The hunt. The *chase*. I should've known that, to a man like Clay, playing God could become an addiction.

Good thing for the two of us—and the rest of the fucking world—that he's already addicted to *me*.

I'll go to my knees for him whenever he wants me to, and if he commands me to crawl to him, I will because nothing gets my husband hotter than thinking he's in control when it comes to sex. I can give him that because, deep down, Clayton Rivers has always been the dog at my feet. I'm his mistress, and he'll do anything to please me.

I say 'fuck', he's already hard. I say 'kill', he won't hesitate to draw his blade. I say 'worship me', and the only man who's ever really loved me for who I am is already on his fucking knees, nuzzling my pussy, begging for a taste.

If it was up to Clay, he'd still be tonguing me now. Sprawled out on the thousand-dollar sheets in the honeymoon suite of our luxury hotel, he gave me two orgasms for breakfast before I shoved him away from me with my foot to his shoulder. As strong as he is, I know he only moved because I wanted him to, and when I motioned for him to flip onto his back so that I could climb on top, he folded his hands behind his back and watched as I fucked him.

But after he finished and the two of us took a shower in the oversized stall—that ended with me bent over under the spray while Clay thumbed my ass as he pounded into my pussy again—I insisted on taking lunch by the glittering infinity pool outside of our hotel.

Clay denies me nothing. He never did while we were married the first time, and now that he's eager to make up those five years to me, I get every fucking thing that I want. I deserve it, too, and maybe when another five years pass, I'll think about easing up the pressure I have on his balls. So he stalked me. So he thought he was giving me what I wanted: another chance at happiness with Tommy. So he never touched another woman while we were separated… He's my husband. I'm his wife.

'Til death do we part.

A small smirk tugs on my lips as I read the last few sentences of that article again, including Detective Jordan's useless plea to get in touch with Aaron; unless he's got a scuba diver and a medium on the GPDs payroll, that's not happening anytime soon. According to the rest of the world, both of us—me and Clay—have died already. But with these new identities, plus enough paperwork and cash to back them up, we've renewed our promises. We've renewed our vows.

We're together, and there is absolutely *nothing* that will ever separate my husband and me again.

Thumbing my phone, I scroll up the top of the page, my smirk turning to a slight frown when I catch a second glance at the picture they used for my 'death' announcement.

I'm amused, but I'm also a vain bitch. "If they're gonna write an article about me dying in such a grisly way, they could've picked a better picture," I mutter, more to myself than to my husband.

As always, though, he hears me.

"You look gorgeous, Cyn," Clay says.

He heard me, but I hear how distracted he suddenly sounds. Glancing over at him, I see his predatory gaze locked on a man seated on the other side of the hotel pool.

Oh, Clay.

The man is a little older than us. I'd put him in his mid-thirties, with a sculpted body he paid for and a hundred-dollar haircut.

He catches my eye. With a tiny smile full of both humor and an undeniable invitation, he pats the empty chair next to him.

Clay starts to get up from his.

The two of us are side by side, lying on a pair of pool chairs that Clay scooted together so that our thighs are touching. It couldn't be more obvious that we're together, and if I'm with a man like Clayton Rivers, I can't imagine why some stranger would think I'd leave my husband for him.

The only exception ever was Tommy Gillis, and that was because the sixteen-year-old Cynthia I once was had a soft spot for him. Even then, I watched him choke on his blood, then framed him for the murders of our entire friend group…

I lay my fingers on top of Clay's arm. He relaxes a fraction, lying back down as he murmurs angrily, "He's been watching you since we came out here."

Because of my skimpy bikini, no doubt. "And?"

Clay's jaw goes tight. "I could carve out his eyes. He'd stop looking at my wife then. Cut off his fingers so he doesn't try to beckon her over to him. Drown him so I feel better. Any of those options work for me."

My heart flutters in my chest. I've forever been the sort of girl who felt butterflies whenever my partner showed his jealous side. It's always turned me on, and if I'm being honest, it's part of the reason I needed Clay and Tommy to choose. One of them had to have loved me more. They needed to *prove* it. To me, seeing that possessiveness, that *jealousy*… to know that my murderous husband would find a knife and do just that to this stranger if I let him… it's not just my heart that's reacting to Clay, either.

I ignore my aching pussy. She already got worked over twice today, and while I'm always ready to welcome my husband, it would probably be better if I distract him before he marches over to the other side of the pool and snaps that guy's neck.

I stroke his arm gently with my fingertips. "Hey. Look at me."

Unable to resist, his eyes are on my face.

"We only just arrived at St. Lucia. You promised me Christmas here. Hard to do that if you maim another guest, babe. Or drown him."

He scowls. "You're mine, Cyn. I don't like the way he's looking at you."

"How about this?" I ask, tossing my phone to the other side of my pool chair. Then, knowing that this will return Clay's attention firmly to me where it belongs, I rise up from my chair and, throwing a leg over his groin, I straddle my husband. "Maybe he likes this view better."

I know Clay does.

His cock is hard beneath my ass. I'm not surprised. He always used to get like this whenever he thought another guy was paying too much attention to me. When we were newly married, he'd find whatever private corner he could just to fuck me and remind himself that I was his.

Another reason why the last five years must have been torture for him, turning him from a blackmailer to a vindictive murderer…

Good. He deserves it for what he put me through, but since I absolutely need this man to be whole myself, I'll look past it so long as he never pulls that shit again.

Tommy had to die. I regret it the tiniest bit, but when I couldn't be sure that Clay's loyalty to his best friend since birth wouldn't fuck up *my* happiness again? This man is mine. His heart. His body. His loyalty.

His *everything*.

And as he relaxes into me, hands going straight to my hips, clinging to me as if remembering the long lonely nights when he watched Tommy have his turn with me… as Clay squeezes me tight, I remind myself that I've *always* owned him—and I wouldn't want it any other way.

He buries his nose in the crook between my shoulder and my neck. Breathing in deep, when he exhales, the rush of warm air on my skin has my nipples pebbling against his chest. "*My wife.*"

I thread my fingers through his hair, jerking his head so that his face is in my cleavage now. His possessive hold on my waist tightens, pulling me even closer.

Releasing his hair, I drape my arms over his shoulders. "You're mine, Clayton," I murmur, low enough that only my husband can hear me. "And if you try to leave me again, I'll fucking kill you myself. No more faking it, babe. You know that. Your only way out of this relationship is in a box."

Clay shudders.

I've told him that before. The night he killed Tommy. When we first left the ferry in Gullhaven and, instead of returning to my home there, immediately started to make plans to head back East. Right after I held down Marla so that Clay could shoot her up with enough heroin that she'd OD before the 'crash'.

I might not have murdered as many as he has, but now we both know where we stand. My mother's murder was on impulse, and Clay encouraged me to finish Chase off, but seeing how much he's enjoying his murderous side… I'll do it. I'll kill him myself before he puts me through that again.

And he knows it.

Even better, knowing that I just threatened *his* life has pushed him from wanting me to *needing* me.

Clay's fingers are nimble and quick. One tug and my bikini bottoms have been shoved over my mound. He dips his pointer finger inside of me, checking to see if I'm ready for him again. Of course I am. Clay mutters my name with a heated groan before shifting his swim shorts down far enough to free his erection.

I rise up on my knees, sinking down on him, wrapping my arms around his neck to complete the connection.

Our hotel is exclusive. Private. We chose this one especially because it is an adult's only resort, and because there aren't as many visitors since it's the week of Thanksgiving back in the States. Apart from us, the only one out by the pool is that man—

I smirk down at my husband. "Is he still watching?"

"Is that bastard watching me fuck my wife?" grunts Clay as he thrusts up into me. His gaze darts to the side, eyes darkening as he grins that boyish grin I fell in love with when I was seventeen. "Oh, yeah."

I dare a quick peek behind me. Instead of patting the pool chair, the stranger has moved his hand to his lap, stroking himself as I slowly swivel my hips, discreetly riding my husband.

"Good. Let him see what no other man will ever have again."

To punctuate my promise, I squeeze—and Clay groans again, forever at my mercy.

And this man really thought he could share me? The five years apart drove him so crazy, he went from my obsessed husband to a masked killer, stalking our old friends for sport in order to keep me for himself. I honestly did him a favor. Tommy, too. If I didn't make Clay choose, he would've eventually snapped and turned on his best friend anyway the first time I fucked Tommy and Clay wasn't involved. I know it to the marrow of my bones, just like how I hate that dead bitch Summer even more knowing that she was fucking Tommy at the same time I was.

Choose? Oh, no. There was never a choice. Not for any of us, but most of all, not for Clayton Rivers.

"God fucking damn it, Cyn, I love you so much," he grates out between clenched teeth. "I never stopped. I never will."

I lean down, tilting my forehead toward his as I grip his shoulders. His eyes are wild. Desperate. I could drown in their depths, and it would be as reckless as shoving my mother's head beneath the water.

Infinitely more satisfying, too.

I grin at my husband.

"Oh, babe, I *know*."

MY WIFE
CARIN HART
"SILLY CYN. YOU SHOULD'VE KNOWN BETTER THAN TO RUN FROM YOUR HUSBAND."
- CLAYTON RIVERS

AUTHOR'S NOTE

Whenever I write a new book, I usually build a Spotify playlist so that I have songs that help me get in the right headspace for the book. I go mainly on vibes. Some songs really capture the story—like Rick Springfield's classic *Jessie's Girl* about a guy in love with his best friends girl—while others just feel right (I'm looking at you, Stevie Nicks). They usually almost feature 80s songs, and this one did more than most others for a very special reason: I was raised on them, thanks to my mom. Like Cyn, my mom is also gone (eight years in February after a long chronic illness), and it was cathartic to write about grief in this book… even if the way we lost our mothers was *very* different.

Still, if you want to get in my head a little after reading this book, I've linked the Spotify playlist here (as well as posting the Spotify code):

And if you've purchased a physical copy of this book, I have special bookmarks and stickers made to give away (as well as a signed bookplate)! Like always, just send me an email with your name and mailing address (to carin@carinhart.com) and I'll get that out ASAP.

Up next: I have a new series starting in 2025, as well as the next **Deal with the Devil** book, releasing in November '24. Keep scrolling/reading/clicking to learn about both *Bloody Wedding* and *Dance with the Devil*.

Until then...

xoxo,
Carin

And I believed that for more than a decade—until I received an invitation to my own wedding.

I thought it was a joke. No way was I going to be forced into marrying one of Owed. It wasn't going to happen—

—and, yet, there I was, dressed in white, about to get married to a man I didn't know.

Whoops. Wrong again.

Because the man who walked in on the ceremony, calmly shooting my 'fiancé' before taking his place?

I know *him*.

Adrian Heller. My biggest tormentor… and my biggest secret.

ADRIAN

For too long, I had to hide how I felt about Loni Dougherty. Considering my obsession with her was the biggest open secret in all of Harmony Heights, I didn't do that great of a job.

Everyone knew—except *her*.

She thought I was her high school bully. And maybe I was, but I also made her untouchable. No one could have her, and I wouldn't let anyone hurt her more than I had to.

But once I became one of the Owed, I could make her mine. I held onto that, too, until she disappeared and my new loyalties meant I couldn't chase her out of town.

That doesn't mean I gave up on her, though. And

when she gets dragged back to Harmony Heights to be given away to another Owed, I make sure the whole order knows that I claimed her first.

She looks so pretty with blood on her wedding dress and my name on her lips, even if her eyes are filled with hate as she vows to be my bride.

But I don't care about that. Loni is mine, and I'll end anyone who tries to take her away from me again.

* *Bloody Wedding* is a dual-POV dark romance that begins the new **The Order of the Owed** series. With the same possessive dark heroes you've met in the **Deal with the Devil** series, and a secret society twist, it gives new meaning to the phrase: *'til death do us part.*

When I meet Cross, my fascination almost becomes an obsession.

As a professional ballerina, it makes sense that I would consider our first few dates a sort of forbidden dance. On the outside, he's everything I'm not: dark, brooding, and—most importantly—a Sinner.

That's right. Damien's little girl fell for a man who wears the mark of his former enemy.

But Cross is no sinner. A sensitive artist who sweeps me off my feet, I want to believe we have a shot to be together. There's a truce now between the Dragonflies and the Sinners' Syndicate, and with Damien settling into wedded bliss with his new bride, I think… maybe. Maybe it's time I show him I'm not that same little girl I used to be.

And that's when I discover just how dark and twisted the Life can be…

CROSS

I've never wanted anything more than I do my butterfly.

I don't care what her last name is. I don't care that, every time I imagine marking up her unblemished, beautiful skin, I'm risking a bullet between my eyes from the head Dragonfly. When I see her, I *feel* for the first time since I was kid who lost everything.

More than that, I'm *inspired*.

Until, one night, everything changes.

I do everything I can to protect her, but when she's

forced to be as brutal as any gangster, my pretty ballerina with the wicked mouth and innocent smile breaks—and, once again, I'm left alone and empty-handed.

But that's the difference between Carlos and Cross. Carlos accepted that fate was cruel and there wasn't anything he could do to change that.

Cross?

He'll burn down all of Springfield to get his Genevieve back.

A modern day retelling of *West Side Story* and *Romeo & Juliet,* what happens when two members of rival syndicates have a chance meeting and sparks fly? Well, if you're tattoo artist Cross and his new muse, Genevieve, you try to stay away from each other — and when that doesn't work, you hope love will be enough to overcome tragedy… and betrayal.

*This is the fourth book in the **Deal with the Devil** series. It tells the story of Genevieve Libellula, the coddled mafia princess, and Carlos "Cross" da Silva, the Sinner artist who has spent his whole life searching for his muse…

KEEP IN TOUCH

Stay tuned for what's coming up next! Follow me at any of these places—or sign up for my newsletter—for news, promotions, upcoming releases, and more:

CarinHart.com
Carin's Newsletter
Carin's Signed Book Store

facebook.com/carinhartbooks
amazon.com/author/carinhart
instagram.com/carinhartbooks

ALSO BY CARIN HART

Deal with the Devil series

No One Has To Know *standalone

Silhouette *standalone

Oubliette *standalone

The Devil's Bargain

The Devil's Bride *newsletter exclusive

The Devil's Playground

Dragonfly

Dance with the Devil

Ride with the Devil

Reed Twins

Close to Midnight

Really Should Stay

The Order of the Owed

Bloody Wedding

Standalone

My Wife